Ben and Leyla—
historical about this! — nevertheless, I hope
that my piece of trivia will afford you some
amusement. With every good wish,
Chris

SINGULARITY

CHRISTOPHER BRYAN

Diamond Press

Singularity

Christopher Bryan

Printed in the United States of America.

The Diamond Press

Proctors Hall Road

Sewanee, Tennessee

For more information about this book, visit:

www.christopherbryanonline.com

Edition ISBNs

Trade Paperback 978-0-9853911-5-7

e-book 978-0-9853911-6-4

Library of Congress Cataloging-in-Publication data is available upon request.

First Edition 2014

This edition was prepared for printing by The Editorial Department

7650 E. Broadway, #308, Tucson, Arizona 85710

www.editorialdepartment.com

Cover design by Pete Garceau

Book design by Christopher Fisher

Diamond Press logo by Richard Posan for Two Ps

In memoriam
Patrick Locke
1934–2012

SINGULARITY

PROLOGUE

9.23 a.m. June 17th, 2001. London.

Sir James Harlow drummed his fingers on the faux-leather upholstery.

He'd been grateful for the ministry car they sent to meet him at Heathrow. But then the morning rush hour turned out to be even heavier than usual, and the journey back to London was taking considerably longer than he or (he imagined) those who arranged his schedule had expected.

He glanced at his watch.

They were surely cutting it fine.

"Should be there any minute now, sir," the driver said. "Sorry it was a bit slow through Hammersmith."

"Nothing you could have done about that. I think you did well, considering."

"Thank you, sir."

As they entered St. James the traffic lightened, and they were soon moving briskly.

Sir James returned to the newspapers in his lap.

"OMAN TRIO FACE DEATH SENTENCE," the *Sun* screamed at him in six-inch type across its front page. "WILL PM CAVE IN?" The *Times* offered a more sober headline: "GOVERNMENT INSISTS OMANI LAW MUST BE UPHELD."

He frowned, shook his head, and sat back in his seat.

They were turning into Southampton Place. The lofty, neo-classical façade of Lancaster House loomed in front of them.

Sir James collected himself and his papers, thanked the driver, and prepared to make a speedy exit.

Minutes later, under the portico, he stopped.

"Damn," he said. "More haste less speed! I've left my second file in the car. And now I *am* running late."

He looked at the two youthful uniformed police officers who were on duty by the main doors.

"I don't suppose…?"

One of them glanced at her companion, who nodded.

"I could run down and get it for you, sir," she said. "If that would help. I know where the driver will have gone."

"Thank you, officer. And you are?"

"Cavaliere, sir. PC Cavaliere."

"Then thank you, Police Constable Cavaliere. It *would* help. It doesn't contain any state secrets, but I need it for reference. Could you ask them to let you bring it to me in there," — he nodded toward Lancaster House — "wherever they take me?"

"Yes, sir."

Some ten or so minutes later Sir James, having received his file, found himself facing the British delegation, led by Charles Haytor, an acquaintance of some years and an experienced civil servant. There were others present whom Sir James did not recognize, as well as a man and a woman whom he rather thought he did — if he were right, fairly senior people from the Secret Intelligence Service (SIS), popularly known as MI6.

"Good morning," he said. "Let's get on with it. As we all know, I'm here at the prime minister's request. So how can I help you?"

Charles Haytor's outline of the situation was much as it was being reported in the media. Charlotte Carmalt-Jones was a young woman working for Carlton Merchant Bankers in the Sultanate of Oman. Fluent in Arabic, she'd been involved in the bank's public relations department for three years. Her younger brother Freddie and his girlfriend Bonnie Carlisle had come out to her for a visit, which would have been no problem had they not brought with them a quantity of marijuana for their personal entertainment — a small matter about which they had not troubled to tell their host. The Omani authorities pulled over Charlotte's car on the way back from the airport to her apartment, discovered the marijuana, and placed the three young people under arrest. As the Omanis made no distinction between "hard" and "soft" drugs, the penalties for illegal possession were likely to involve heavy prison sentences and had on occasion even stretched to the death penalty.

"Frankly," Haytor concluded, "the PM's anxious to get this over with. Oman's strategically important to us, and our relationship with the Sultanate is generally good. He wants it to stay that way. The Carmalt-Jones girl says she didn't know a thing about the marijuana, and the Omanis seem to believe her. They'd be willing to let her get on a plane home any time she likes — or of course stay in Oman if she wishes. But they're not budging on her brother and his girlfriend, who knowingly flouted Omani law and must stand trial. Of course if you can come up with something that'll get us a better deal *fast*, the PM will be grateful. Otherwise, he's going to take what the Omanis are offering and live with it, regardless of fallout. So — do you think you can help?"

Sir James looked round the table.

"Perhaps," he said. "But I'm not sure who is supposed to know what. May I talk to you alone for a minute? Oh — you Secret Intelligence people can stay if you want. Actually, it might be useful if you did. You *are* SIS, aren't you?"

The two looked irritated but did not deny it.

Charles Haytor nodded.

Within minutes the room was clear except for Sir James, Haytor, and the two from SIS.

Sir James nodded. "Good. Now—have you given me all the facts about the situation?"

"You've seen the materials. Have you something else in mind that we should give you?"

"Let me put it another way. Are you quite sure there isn't something about all this that you aren't telling me?"

"James, why on earth would you think that?"

"Well, to start with, Charles, I'd think it because you've just twice evaded giving a direct answer to my question. And the second time you did it, you glanced at our SIS friends here, all of which tells me you and they know something you think I don't know."

If Charles Haytor looked embarrassed, it was only slightly, and very briefly.

"Now," Sir James said, "by way of clearing the decks, I'm going to tell you what I think *I* know, after looking at the videos and the other stuff you've given me. Under questioning, Charlotte Carmalt-Jones says she knew nothing about the drugs. It's evident the Omanis believe her, and so do I. Apart from anything else, she's obviously far too intelligent to have anything to do with anything so stupid—in marked contrast to Freddie Carmalt-Jones, her evidently empty-headed brother, and his nitwit girlfriend. And incidentally, regardless of whatever Islamophobic tripe the media may be serving up, I think we here can all agree that the Omanis' interview with Charlotte was conducted with courtesy and full respect for her rights under international law."

He paused.

"So, I believe she's telling the truth about *that*—her involvement, or rather non-involvement, with the drugs. Where she *did* seem evasive, though, was when the interviewer asked her about her employment. It wasn't anything much. She's good. I can see why he didn't pick it up. It was the drugs he was interested in, not where she worked. But *I* noticed it because I was paying attention to everything.

"Then of course there's what happened when the three went on television yesterday and apologized to the Omani people. Charlotte slurred certain words, which has the media screaming 'sleep-deprivation.' But we in this room all know that was really just Charlotte using intelligence service code to say, 'I'm fine. They haven't broken my cover yet,' don't we?"

He paused again and gazed at the two from SIS, who gazed back.

He nodded.

"Good," he said, "I'm glad we're all agreed. In other words, lady and gentlemen, our Charlotte is spying for us, and we need her to be safe at home before the Omanis decide to start seriously investigating her. Because if they do, and if they realize what she's really up to, then they will be *royally* pissed and we don't want that to happen, do we? And *that's* why the PM will take any deal he can get, just so long as we get her out of there fast. Yes?"

The room was silent.

Haytor looked at the other two, who shrugged. He looked back at Sir James.

"That's about it," he said.

"Good. So now, Charles, is there anything *else* you aren't telling me? Because I can't work with you people if I don't know what you know. And frankly, old boy, it's bloody foolish to expect me to. Forgive my bluntness, but I've been studying the stuff you sent me all night on the plane, I've come straight from the airport, and I'm not in the best of moods."

Charles Haytor smiled.

"Jimmy Harlow, even jetlagged you're a damned sight too clever for your own good. No, there isn't anything else we're not telling you. At least, not so far as I know."

Sir James stared at him for several seconds, then nodded.

"All right, Charles, I believe you. Now, here's the first thing you need to do."

Some twenty minutes later the two delegations again sat facing each other. Charles Haytor reopened proceedings on behalf of Her Majesty's government, stating essentially the same British request as yesterday: that in view of their youth and their apology to the Omani people, the three young people should be released at once into British custody. The negotiator facing him looked understandably somewhat irritated by this repetition, but then, as he rose to restate the Omani position, Haytor made his surprise move. Rising to his feet, and looking past the Omani negotiator, he addressed himself directly to a slim, elegant young man standing behind the negotiator and slightly to his right.

"Greatly as we appreciate the wisdom and courtesy over this distressing affair that have so far been expressed by *all* members of the Omani delegation," Haytor said, "I believe that at this point Her Majesty's government would be grateful if it might hear directly from Doctor Fadal himself his view of the British proposals."

The slim young man looked surprised for only a moment. He then signaled for the Omani negotiator to be seated, drew himself up to his full height, and began his reply.

At the end of which Charles Haytor thanked him graciously and asked for a recess during which the British delegation might consider his views.

"Two questions," Haytor said when he was back with Sir James. "How the devil did you know he was the head man, and what good has it done us?"

"The first one's easy," Sir James said. "When their delegation arrives, he's always the one who comes in last, which in that culture clearly says that he's the most important. The second's trickier, but I think we may have something. As soon as I was sure he was the man, I had my people start researching him. Here's what we've got. He's a good politician, but his family's not as powerful as it might be. He's clever — which is why they gave him this job — but he still tends to get handed the stuff no one else wants to do. What he'd like is a situation in which his people would see him as a leader taken seriously on the world stage. Did you notice how he drew himself up when he started to speak? He wants to be bigger! Now here's what I suggest you do."

He leaned forward and spoke rapidly.

"Good God, you don't ask much!" Haytor said when he'd finished.

Sir James swallowed a smile.

When the delegations reassembled at 3.00 pm, Charles Haytor began with the minimum of preliminaries.

"Her Majesty's government will appreciate His Majesty the Sultan of Oman's graciousness and clemency in granting a full pardon to the three British subjects in Omani custody. In token of this appreciation, the prime minister of Great Britain wishes Doctor Fadal to accept this on behalf of Her Majesty's government."

A secretary to the British delegation came forward and laid a large, impressive looking envelope on the table in front of Doctor Fadal, who frowned slightly, then opened it and read the contents.

There was a pause.

Slowly, the faintest of smiles came to his lips.

He nodded.

"PC Cavaliere!" Sir James paused at the entrance as he left

Lancaster House, turning aside from the group that was accompanying him. "Still on duty?"

"I had a break for lunch, sir."

"Well, I'm glad to hear it. Anyway, you fetched my documents for me this morning and thereby saved me from looking like a complete idiot! I just wanted to thank you."

"I was happy to help, sir."

"Your name sounds Italian to me. Yet your voice has a hint of Devon in it, I think. I'm a Devon man myself."

"I imagine I do have a bit of Devon, sir. I grew up in Exeter and my father teaches classics at the university. But our family is Italian."

"*Lei parla italiano?*"

"*Sì, Sir James. Sempre a casa parliamo italiano.*"

"Ah — without accent, I think. You are bilingual."

"Yes, sir."

"Wonderful. I envy you. Well, thank you again for your help. I think that between us all we may have had a successful day."

"That's great news, sir. I'm glad things went well."

"Sir James Harlow seems nice," PC Cecilia Cavaliere said to her father, talking that evening on the telephone. "He actually remembered I was the one who'd fetched his file and stopped to thank me on his way out. And I don't know what he did in those negotiations, but he seems to have got the three of them off scot-free. Did you see it on the news? So far as I could see, last night each side was calling the other names and striking attitudes. Tonight it's all handshakes, new eras of cooperation between Britain and Oman, and princely pardons for suitably apologetic delinquents as if no one had ever thought of doing anything else."

"Ah, well," Papa said, "it just goes to show what can be achieved at the right moment by the offer of a state dinner in your honor and a knighthood. The English may not have an empire anymore, but it's amazing to me how often they still manage to pull off acting as if they did!"

ONE

Twelve years later.
2:10 p.m. Thursday, 22nd August, 2013.
A few miles east of Exeter.

B ill Frasier applied the van's brakes yet again and swore loudly. This section of the A30 was more or less up to motorway standard, and he'd expected to be able to get a move on. But not a hope! The traffic was moving more slowly than ever, and he'd been in the middle of a crawl pretty well all the way from Newhaven. Just his luck, of course. The weather had been fine and hot for weeks — a heat wave, they called it — and now on the one day when he had to drive it rained. And such rain! It was pelting. A deluge. The windscreen wipers were racing and even so could hardly cope. He peered at the satnav. Still over fifty miles to go! He was supposed to deliver his cargo by two, and at this rate there was no way he was going to be there by three-thirty. He muttered a fresh obscenity, then pulled out into the fast lane and accelerated past the line of cars.

There was a white van ahead. He could see its taillights, and it seemed to be going at a reasonable lick. He settled in behind it and glanced down to reach for his cigarettes. When he looked up again he wasn't seeing the white van's taillights but its side, directly ahead of him, shining in his headlights and the rain. "Acme Environmental Solutions" it said, big green letters rushing at him out of the deluge. He applied the brakes. Which were completely useless. He was aquaplaning.

He heard the crash as if from a great distance but he didn't feel a thing.

Quite what had happened or how long he'd been sitting there he wasn't sure, but his vehicle wasn't moving anymore and it was facing the wrong way. The windscreen wipers were still working, though, and through driving rain he could see an overturned car and another on its side.

He had a terrible headache. Like he'd had that time after the fight. He must have hit his head on something.

He tried to open the driver's side door. Jammed. What if he was trapped and the petrol tank blew up? In sudden panic he unfastened his safety belt and wriggled across to the passenger door—it opened okay and he staggered out into the rain, which for a moment felt cool and refreshing. And at least he didn't seem to have broken any bones.

There was the white Acme van over on its side. No one was stirring in it. As for the van he'd been driving—his brother's van—the drivers' side headlight and the wing were all smashed in. Chuck would blow a gasket when he saw.

He could hear groans and cries for help ahead of him. Back down the road people were getting out of their vehicles, some of them trying to help other people.

And now he could hear sirens. The police and the emergency services were on their way.

Shit!

If the cops caught him here with what he was carrying, he'd be doing time forever.

It was time to scarper.

His head was splitting, but he couldn't do anything about that now. For now he had to get away from here, and alongside the road there was a steep wet bank. Crap!

He managed, barely, to climb the bank—slipping and cursing in grass and mud as he went—then walked along the edge of a muddy field, and at last came to a narrow lane with tall hedges on either side.

He walked along that for a few yards, head still throbbing, and then thought of his mobile phone.

He could call them.

They'd help.

They'd have to. After all, he was working for them.

He pulled the phone out of his pocket and stabbed in a number.

"It's Bill Frasier," he said.

"*Frasier*! What the hell do you mean by calling me here?"

"There's been a crash." He explained what had happened as best he could.

"Okay. Well I guess you were right to get away from the van. There's nothing in it that links it to us, I hope."

"I don't think so."

"Good. Well I don't have a goddamn clue where you are and it sounds as if you don't either. Have you any money?"

"Yeah. A bit."

"Okay. Stick to the lanes and keep walking. You're bound to come to a village sooner or later and there'll be a pub. I think you Brits have more pubs than people. Then call me from it and tell me where you are and I'll send someone to get you. And this time use the pub's phone, its landline, not your cell. Is that clear?"

"Yeah."

"Well, get on with it, then."

Bill Frasier walked on into the rain, which was no longer refreshing—just cold. He was soaked to the skin.

His head was pounding. He felt sick and dizzy.

He stumbled but managed to recover, then kept on his way. He hoped he came to a village soon.

TWO

Exeter, Devon. Friday, 23rd August, 2013. 7:30 a.m.

Saint Mary's rectory was an enormous, sprawling place, handsome in its own way but easy to get lost in. The Victorian architect who designed it obviously expected the parish priest and his wife to have lots of servants and lots of babies. Detective Inspector Cecilia Anna Maria Cavaliere and Father Michael Aarons had no servants (although they did employ Lucretia and Lisa, who came into the rectory for several hours a week and worked wonders) and they had so far managed one baby: Rachel Rosina Maria, a princess who would no doubt one day rule the galaxy.

At three years old, Rachel showed every sign of inheriting Cecilia's and Michael's interest in food, so meals with her were never a speedy affair. On this particular morning breakfast was made especially long by the need to discuss in great detail a brown bunny, who had appeared on the lawn yesterday morning and then reappeared with a little friend in the evening. Their dog Figaro (who was supervising breakfast from a patch of sun on a rug by the French windows, and thumped his tail at every mention of his name) had been as interested in the bunny as Rachel — although, as she was quite clever enough to understand, not at all for the same reason. All this, accompanied by much giggling and dramatic gesture, took considerable time to describe — not least because everything had to be said in two languages.

They'd decided from the beginning that Cecilia would speak with Rachel in Italian, and Michael in English, in the hope that she would emerge from this process as happily bilingual as Cecilia herself. The plan seemed to be working, with the unexpected consequence that whenever Rachel said something to one parent in one language, she never seemed quite to believe that the other parent had got it, and so would repeat it word for word in the other's language.

"In short," Cecilia said to Michael soon after they first noticed this phenomenon, "she appears to be becoming not just bilingual but a bilingual pain."

"Perhaps," Michael said, "we have produced a prodigy."

"I dare say we'll know when people start congratulating us about her."

"At the same time no doubt congratulating themselves that their own children are developing along more normal lines!"

Breakfast was almost — finally — over when a moment of high drama was provided by a wasp, who must have been dormant in the room overnight and was now roused to action by the marmalade on Rachel's toast. Michael had a method for getting such flying creatures out of the house. It involved a glass tumbler, a piece of card, and (according to him) an enormous amount of skill, patience, and cunning. All this took several minutes, but eventually the wasp was restored to its natural habitat where, Michael assured it as it flew off amid cries of "Bravo! Bravissimo!" from Rachel and Cecilia, "despite the absence of Rachel's marmalade, you will in the long run be a great deal happier, and so will we."

By the time Cecilia and Michael kissed each other goodbye, Cecilia kissed Rachel, Michael went to his study to work on the parish newsletter, and Cecilia left for the Heavitree Police Station — by the time all this happened, Rosina Cavaliere,

Cecilia's mother, who was looking after Rachel for the day, had already been in the house for nearly an hour and was evidently thinking of making for herself a second *caffè*.

Cecilia had an appointment with the chief superintendent — for which, she realized as she got into the car, she was going to be late.

She *was* late.

But before she could apologize, Chief Superintendent Glyn Davies, who was signing letters when she entered his office and did not seem to have noticed the time, said "Good morning, Cavaliere," motioned her to a chair, and pointed to the latest *Express and Echo* on his desk.

"RIOT IN EDGESTOW," the headline said.

"You've seen that, of course."

"I heard about it, sir."

"We've got a problem." He signed another letter, put down his pen, and sat back in his chair. "It would appear," he said, "that the prime minister is heavily onto the back of the responsible minister to do something about it, and *she's* heavily onto the chief constable's back, and now *he* is heavily onto *my* back."

"Yes, sir."

"Cavaliere, Edgestow has to be sorted."

"Yes, sir."

Edgestow, seventy or so miles from Exeter, was on paper little more than a collection of houses and a few shops adjacent to a stretch of land occasionally used by the Ministry of Defence for military exercises. But there was more to it than that. The houses and shops were what remained of a medium-sized town and a small medieval university, both destroyed by a freak earthquake in 1945. Following the earthquake, local legend had it that the area once occupied by the university and the main part of the town was ill-omened, even cursed. Science had it that the land was geologically unstable, good for nothing save the occasional military jaunt.

Either way, no one wanted to be there. And that was how it had been, ever since Cecilia could remember.

Except that in the last few months all that had changed.

A government-commissioned investigation and report by the British Geological Survey declared that the site was safe. Future generations might build upon it.

And so it was to be.

To the delight of Her Majesty's government, after much international jockeying, after bids and counter-bids and coun-ter-counter-bids, a deal had been struck. The United Nations Institute for Technological Experimentation and Development ("U.N.I.T.E.D.") was coming to Edgestow. Its development plans for the site were extensive, and were backed by what appeared to be limitless funds. If there were one or two voices suggesting that the proposed *level* of development ignored some rather significant reservations in the BGS report—if there were such voices, they received little notice. U.N.I.T.E.D. was bringing jobs to the work force, foreign capital to the economy, and prestige to the nation.

Even so, U.N.I.T.E.D. had created a problem.

One constable, with occasional support from Exeter, had been entirely sufficient to maintain the Queen's peace in the remnants of Edgestow and the village of St. Anne's-on-the-Hill from 1945 to 2013. But one constable could hardly be expected to do that for the enlarged community now emerg-ing. Eventually a separate department was to be set up. A new police headquarters had been commissioned, and permanent officers under their own superintendent would staff it.

But to set all that in order would take time.

And in the meantime there were tensions between newcom-ers and local inhabitants. There had been brawls in a couple of pubs—the last, on the previous Monday evening, so seri-ous that it had been necessary to bring in police from Exeter to calm the situation. That was the "riot" to which the *Express and Echo*'s headline referred — an exaggeration, of course, but not so much of an exaggeration that those responsible for law and order could afford to ignore it.

"Well, Cavaliere," the chief superintendent said, "here's what's going to happen. For the next three months — until they get that new station up and running — I'm arranging for a detective inspector from here, together with a detective sergeant, eight uniformed constables, and a uniformed sergeant, to serve Edgestow from a temporary headquarters. The uniformed officers for general police duties, the two detectives available for anything more serious.

"The detective inspector will have the acting rank of detective *chief* inspector, to give more seniority, and if the operation's a success that rank will become permanent at the end of it. I'm also going to provide a couple of civilians, one computer specialist and a secretary. And I want the whole thing up and running by the end of next week. No messing around. We need to get this done."

Cecilia nodded.

She could be flattering herself, but she rather thought she saw where all this might be going.

"The chief constable's given his okay, and he and Sir James Harlow have agreed to give a joint interview about it all on television this evening. Soothing words for the populace, I hope."

"Yes, sir."

Sir James Harlow had been appointed by the government to head up U.N.I.T.E.D. Cecilia had, of course, her own good recollection of Sir James from their brief encounter at Lancaster House ten or so years ago. Then, as it happened, she'd met him again only a few weeks ago when she was with Michael at a fund-raising dinner in aid of Syrian refugees. She, at least, had been as impressed with him as ever.

But Sir James Harlow's agreeing to take on the U.N.I.T.E.D. position had surprised her when she read about it. Though the institute could hardly have better leadership during its early days, heading it seemed trivial for a man widely acknowledged to have been the guiding hand behind the peaceful solution of more than one international crisis over the last two decades, beginning with the NATO intervention in Bosnia in 1993. Even now he was rumored to be working to bring about some resolution to the Syrian crisis.

Her mind had wandered. She returned her attention to the chief superintendent.

"So the only question is, who's going to be the detective inspector — that's to say the detective *chief* inspector — in charge down there? The point is, I'd like it to be you, Cavaliere. I'm not ordering you — I know you've got a three-year-old — but if you could make it work you're the one I'd send. And for obvious reasons I need you to decide quickly. In fact by tomorrow morning, first thing. I see you're off duty then — so you'd best phone me here. Can you do that?"

So he *did* want her to do it.

And of course that pleased her.

"Yes, sir, I can phone you," she said. "First thing tomorrow morning."

But she rather thought her decision wouldn't be the one he wanted.

THREE

Saint Mary's Rectory. That evening.

"Of course it's nice to have been asked," she said, when she and Michael were with her parents Andrea and Rosina that evening after Rachel had gone to bed. "But I don't think I want to do it."

"Why on earth wouldn't you?" Michael said. "Davies is paying you a colossal and well-deserved compliment. He obviously thinks you're the best person for the job. Don't you?"

He knew her so well! She swallowed a smile.

"Well, yes. But for one thing it would mean leaving you alone to look after Rachel, not to mention running the parish. Which just isn't on."

"We could make it work. Your mama and papa have already said they'd move into the rectory to help with Rachel — at least there are some advantages to living in a huge house!"

"Lares and Penates could be honored in your absence," her father said, "and the home fires kept burning."

Cecilia smiled, gently amused at Papa's mixture of Roman piety and British jingoism.

As for the point he was making...

She hesitated.

She frowned.

"Out with it, then," Michael said.

He knew her *too* well.

"All right," she said, "it isn't just that I don't want to be away from you and Rachel for twelve weeks, though I don't. The truth is, I really don't want to be in Edgestow that long — or at all, for that matter. I suppose I've grown up with negative feelings about the place. *Bad* feelings. I dare say it's not rational, but the fact is I just don't want to go."

Michael sighed.

"Well," he said, "I can't argue with that."

Neither of them said anything for a minute. It was Michael who broke the silence.

"But I must say, while I respect your instincts, and I don't think mere reason can get us everywhere we need to go" — Cecilia sensed he was choosing his words carefully — "I'm always a bit worried if my *only* basis for doing or not doing something seems actually to be *ir*rational."

She stared at him, he stared back.

And so, by mutual consent, they let it rest.

Half an hour or so later they sat together in front of the television and watched BBC Southwest's *Spotlight* as the chief constable of Devon and Cornwall and Sir James Harlow were interviewed about "the situation at Edgestow." Sir James spoke of "inevitable" tensions and misunderstandings caused by the influx of so many new people and communities into an area rich in its own history and traditions. He and the chief constable agreed that such tensions were "to be expected" and were "no one's fault." Finally the chief constable expressed his hope that the low key presence of a few extra police officers in Edgestow would help all parties in smoothing out these "unavoidable" teething troubles.

"Sir James speaks well," Papa said when it was over. "Unusually so for a modern politician."

"He does speak well," Michael said.

And stopped.

Cecilia looked at him but found his face hard to read. She thought back to the fundraising banquet organized by the cathedral and diocesan clergy where they'd met Sir James — who was there because he was, among other things, a lay reader in the Church of England. They were introduced to him over drinks before the banquet started, and she'd found him to be much as she remembered him — a little plumper in the face, perhaps, but still a fine-looking man with a twinkle in his eye. When someone complimented him on his being willing to accept the burden of heading up U.N.I.T.E.D., he said that on the contrary it was an honor and pleasure for him, just for once, to be doing something for Devon, the county he loved and that was his home, as opposed to rushing about the globe.

Cecilia would not have dared mention her own brief meeting with him all those years ago, but Sir James had no such qualms.

"Forgive me," he said, "I fear this may sound like an old man trying to use the oldest line in the book, but I have to ask — haven't you and I met somewhere before?"

She laughed.

"Actually, we have. Just for a few minutes! Do you remember an affair you were involved in some years ago — when three of our people were arrested for carrying drugs in Oman?"

He hesitated for a second, then broke into a broad smile.

"Oh my God! Yes, I do! And now I know who you are — you're the police officer on the steps at Lancaster House who fetched my file and saved me from looking like an idiot. Police Constable Cavaliere."

Cecilia smiled and nodded.

"That was me," she said.

She was impressed that he had remembered her after such a brief encounter so long ago. Impressed and — she could hardly deny it — more than a little flattered.

Later in the conversation she asked him about his famed negotiating skills.

He shook his head and smiled.

"It's mostly a matter of paying attention — listening carefully and getting people to listen to each other," he said.

"Though I imagine that a lot of the people you work with don't *want* to listen to each other?"

"That's true, certainly. And if they persist in that attitude then there's nothing much I or anyone else can do about it." He paused, reflecting. "Even then, sometimes just the fact they've faced each other across a table is of some value. Winston Churchill said that even if international negotiations were just jaw-jaw, still that was better than war-war. I think he was right."

"I imagine," Michael said, "that even if it's only jaw-jaw, the mere ritual of negotiation — coming to the special place to meet, the unavoidable recognition of each other's existence and therefore in some sense of each other's rights, having to follow the rules — all that play of ceremony must have *some* civilizing effect, even if those performing it know they're telling lies. *Homo ludens* and all that."

"You're absolutely right," Sir James said. "I've watched it happen, again and again." He paused. "If as a result of all this they actually *do* start to talk seriously to each other about what really concerns them, then quite often my task — and my challenge — is to listen hard to both sides myself. If you pay attention you can frequently see things going on with people that they aren't at all willing to admit, or aren't able to admit, or don't even know themselves. As I recall, paying attention was one of the keys to solving that Omani business." He smiled at Cecilia. "And sometimes the people who are negotiating are actually coming up with their own solutions to their problems without realizing it. My job then is to point that out to them."

"That," Michael said, "sounds to me a lot like hearing confessions, at least in the Anglican tradition. It's important to listen closely to everything the penitent says and how the confession is made, because in doing so you can often come to understand how best to counsel them. Quite frequently, entirely without realizing it, the penitents themselves are telling you what they need to be told."

Sir James looked hard at him, and Michael returned his gaze. For a moment Cecilia had the odd impression that the two of them were quite apart from everyone else in the room, feeling each other out, testing one another.

Then Sir James nodded again.

"Yes," he said. "That's just how it is. I believe, Father, that you must be a very good confessor."

It was Michael's turn to shake his head, and smile.

"Is that beautiful little Harlow House I've noticed in the cathedral close connected with your family?" Cecilia asked as they walked in to dinner.

Sir James laughed.

"Indeed it is. How observant of you! It's eighteenth century, of course, but it's only been in our family since the middle of the nineteenth. Believe it or not, my great-great-grandfather had the nerve to buy it and set up his beautiful mistress in it—in full of view of the cathedral! And that was precisely the point. It was conveniently placed so she could walk to church on Sunday to attend services, which apparently she liked to do."

"Good heavens!"

"And you're right. It *is* a beautiful little house. I love Marsden Hall, of course, but Harlow House is the private spot where I go and contemplate the cathedral whenever I've got something big to deal with. It's got a stunning view of the west end, and it's the perfect place to ask yourself, where do I go from here?"

As the banquet was about to begin, the Bishop, magnificent in purple, rose to his feet and in the silence that followed craved leave, before saying grace, to make an announcement. Sir James Harlow, he informed them, had just graciously undertaken to match from his own resources whatever sums the fundraising banquet and its associated events succeeded in raising, so in effect doubling the value of every single pound donated on behalf of the Syrian refugees. The Bishop was sure that all present would wish to join him in expressing their appreciation to Sir James for this splendid act of munificence and generosity.

Cecilia rose to her feet as did everyone else, and applauded enthusiastically.

She'd found much to enjoy in their meeting with Sir James. But she'd also read Michael's reaction to him.

"You don't like him," she said when they got home.

He smiled.

"Why do you say that? I hope I wasn't rude."

"No, of course you weren't. Actually, you were very polite. And I think he was really interested in what you said. But I know you. You don't like him."

He sighed.

"Oh, Lord! It's hard to go against the opinion of the world. *Orbis terrarum* and all that!" He chuckled. "But I admit it. It's not exactly that I don't like him, and I know you have good feelings about him, which is important to me—I've seen more than once what a good judge of people you are. But still, there is something about him that disturbs me. When you were talking to him, I had the oddest impression you were talking to two people. It's as if from time to time—in a gesture, an expression—a mask slipped, or a different mask replaced it. And I didn't know what that meant, or which mask was real—or if either was."

"Still think he's two people?" she said quietly to Michael when the television interview was over.

"Maybe… I still find some things about him disturbing. But I can't put a precise finger on them, and he does talk sense."

"So as I understand it, I'm to take seriously your negative reaction to Sir James, even though you 'can't put a precise finger' on your reasons for it. But you find it hard to take seriously my negative reaction to Edgestow, because I can't put a precise finger on my reason for that?"

Papa glanced at his watch.

"I think," he said to Mama, "it's time for us to be going. I should look at my class notes for tomorrow."

"And I need to be getting back too. Don't you two bother! We can see ourselves out. Come along, Pu! Tocco!"

There were goodnights and see-you-tomorrows, then Cecilia and Michael were alone.

Cecilia again had the impression he was choosing his words carefully when he finally spoke.

"I don't think we should ever simply ignore our feelings about things," he said, "whether we can see reasons for them or not. But I also think that if we *can't* see reasons for them, we ought at least to be cautious about using our feelings alone as a basis for action — or inaction."

He hesitated — in fact his hesitation was so lengthy that she ended it.

"So?" she said.

"Well, I was going to drop it, and I will drop it if you tell me to, but here's the thing. Although I do have negative feelings about Sir James, since I don't have reasons for them that are easily explainable even to me, I'm trying to keep an open mind. To put it another way, the world may be right about him and I may be wrong. As for Edgestow, since your reasons for objecting to the place also aren't very clear, maybe you too should keep an open mind. Maybe you should ask yourself whether the UN and the British Geological Survey could be right and you could be wrong. Which translates, I suppose, into, maybe you ought to think a bit more about the Edgestow job and the possibilities it offers before you turn it down."

She stared at him.

He looked so serious that despite herself she felt her lips twitching into a smile.

"You wouldn't by any chance be trying to get rid of me for three months, would you, sir?"

"No I damn well wouldn't and you know it."

Of course she knew it.

She sighed.

Michael and her parents could manage while she was away. That she'd never doubted. And surely there were things about the job offer that appealed to her. The promotion did, obviously. And she relished the prospect of new challenges. It would be fun, too, to be captain of her own ship, even if it was only a little one and only for a few months.

Her essential problem was exactly as she'd stated it: she had bad feelings about being in Edgestow.

But how rational was that?

What we can't show, we don't know. Edgestow was, after all, just a town, whatever its history. And apparently it needed something that she had to give.

She gave a sigh.

"I'll think about it," she said. "And now for God's sake let us go to bed."

FOUR

Cecilia got up early the following morning, made herself coffee, and sat alone in the cool light of dawn, drinking the coffee and thinking about Edgestow just as she had promised.

And after thinking about it for close to an hour, she knew what she was going to do. Right or wrong, she felt better for having come to a decision.

"Thank God for that," the chief superintendent said when she phoned him. "Frankly, I thought you were going to say no and I didn't want to twist your arm. But I really do think you're the one for this job. Now as I said, you're to have the acting rank of detective chief inspector—to become substantive on your return to Exeter. You'll assume that rank immediately."

"Thank you very much, sir."

"No need to thank anyone! Everyone thinks you've earned it, including me. Now, pick your team following the guidelines I indicated, and providing you don't choose someone who's indispensible here, I'll let you have them. Everyone needs to be willing to move by the middle of next week."

Glyn Davies replaced the phone, sat back in his chair, and nodded with satisfaction. Given Cavaliere's family background—on her father's side she came, he gathered, from generations of service with the Italian *Carabiniere*—perhaps her professionalism was innate. In the genes, so to speak. But whether it was in the genes or not, DI Cavaliere—or rather, as she would now be, DCI Cavaliere—had it. And that quality, in his view, made her at this moment exactly what the problems of Edgestow needed.

Naturally Cecilia's first choice for an officer to be with her from CID was DS Verity Jones, a younger colleague who over the last three or four years had not only been her valued assistant in a number of cases but had also become her trusted friend.

The presence of an older man on the team would be an invaluable source of the kind of wisdom that can only come from experience, and Sergeant Wyatt, who was close to retirement, would be ideal. She thought at first that he'd be reluctant to leave Exeter for three months—but no, when she phoned him it turned out that Mrs. Wyatt had just gone to stay with her married sister in Marseilles for ten weeks, so the tour of duty in Edgestow couldn't have been more conveniently timed.

With the sergeant's help Cecilia chose eight of the younger constables, who were without households and open to adventures, and a secretary.

And of course they would need her Bahamian friend, computer specialist Joseph Stirrup. He was eager to oblige, not only because he was fascinated by the prospects for U.N.I.T.E.D.'s work and looked forward to being in closer proximity to what was going on, but also, and perhaps especially, because Verity Jones would be there.

When Cecilia phoned through her choices to Chief Superintendent Davies late on Saturday afternoon, he approved them all.

"I'll pass the names straight over to admin," he said, "and they can get on with seeing you're all fixed up with digs."

"It'll be a bit short notice, won't it, sir?"

"Yes it will," he said, "but that won't matter. I've already made some inquiries. Luckily for us it's near the end of the season. There's plenty of B&Bs will fall over themselves for a twelve week let at this time of year, short notice or not."

FIVE

In the days that remained before she was to leave Exeter, Cecilia determined to learn everything she could of Edgestow generally and, of course, of U.N.I.T.E.D. A mere half-hour's research was enough to reveal that the number and scope of projects to be initiated or sustained by the institute was staggering. The environment, world health, and the problem of renewable fuels were just three of the areas where new developments were to be explored and assessed.

Joseph Stirrup, as she would have expected, was especially excited about the developments in computing likely to emerge. Indeed, he was so energized that he could not restrain himself from walking about the room as he explained them to her—which was a delight in itself, since until little over a year ago he'd been confined to a wheel chair. Surgery followed by extensive physiotherapy had got him to the point where he was able to get about quite well with a stick—which at this moment he evidently found also invaluable for emphasizing his points.

"Computers aren't just getting faster," he said, "they're getting faster *faster*. Your mobile phone is a fraction the size of the computer that was regarded as hi-tech at MIT forty years ago, a fraction its cost, and yet a thousand times more powerful.

Fast forward that progression, and what have you got? We've already built a computer no human being can beat at chess. Soon we'll have a computer that's superior to us in a whole range of respects—quicker to calculate, perfect retention of data, and so on. In other words, the super intelligent android, like Commander Data in *Star Trek*, isn't nearly so far away or fantastical as most people think."

"So—why's the U.N. involved? It seems we're getting there without them."

"That all depends on what you mean by 'we.' So far the major supercomputers all belong to individual nations like China or the United States, or in the case of the Eurozone, a group of wealthy industrialized nations. But when we get to the *super* supercomputer, wouldn't it be nice if it belonged to the *world*, so that *everyone* had a chance to benefit from what it could do? That's where the U.N. comes in. U.N.I.T.E.D.'s going to be provided with the resources to build that computer, and not just one rich nation or group of rich nations but the *world* will have access to it. That's what I hope, anyway."

The internal workings of the institute were not expected to constitute a problem for the police, since U.N.I.T.E.D. was to have its own security, which would be formidable. In the interests of international cooperation a Latvian company had been hired: Eglītis, which had a reputation for being both tough and efficient. Personnel working for private security firms are not allowed to carry firearms in the United Kingdom, but in this case—and against the advice of the Devon and Cornwall police—the government had agreed to make an exception.

The chief superintendent, Cecilia discovered, was particularly annoyed about this.

"The home secretary must be off his head. Within the institute's grounds they're to be allowed to carry MP5s, *exactly the same weapons as we use*. It's a disgrace. Next thing we know, we'll have the same mess here as they've got in the United States."

Cecilia allowed for some hyperbole here. There was a way to go before the situation in Britain became as bad as that in the U.S., where half the time, so far as she could see, the crooks appeared to be better armed than the police. Still, on the main point she agreed with him.

"The government wanted to get the institute on the site and up and running, I suppose," she said.

"Damned right they did. They were so damned anxious to get them here they'd have agreed to anything."

Six

Preparations for Cecilia's departure went smoothly enough. She and Michael explained carefully to Rachel that Mummy would have to be away for some weeks because of her work. But she would be at home every other weekend, and Daddy and Grandpapa and Grandmamma would be there all the time to look after her.

And Rachel seemed to accept all this with equanimity — until it was time for Cecilia to leave.

At which point Rachel hurled herself at her mother and clung to her, begging her not to go.

"*Mamma, mamma, non andare!*"

Cecilia looked at Michael, bewildered.

She and Michael again did their best to reassure their daughter, repeating all the things they'd already told her. But everything they said, in Italian or in English, was interrupted by sobs.

"I don't *want* Mummy to go! *Mamma, mamma, non andare!*"

It didn't help that Cecilia then began crying herself. Rachel had never before been so upset — over anything.

At which point, gently but firmly, Michael somehow managed to untangle the weeping child from her weeping mother, calm the tears of both, and — still holding his daughter — get his wife into the car.

"Thank you, darling," she said through the open car window and tears that continued to flow. "There are moments when I really know why I married you."

He grinned at her.

"Good!" he said. "Hold that thought! And drive carefully. I definitely want you back."

SEVEN

Several miles west of Exeter, sometime later.

A new motorway-style extension running north from the A30 had been constructed (with something like record speed) specifically to serve the institute. But Cecilia chose instead the relative peace of country roads. She left the A30 by the B3260 exit towards Okehampton and then drove slowly north from Okehampton to the village of Petrockstowe, where she discovered a village green with a flagpole flying the cross of Saint George—the English flag, she noted, not that of the Union. Beyond the green was a medieval church and beside it a seventeenth-century pub called The Laurels.

The Laurels was serving lunch—at which sight it occurred to Cecilia that she was hungry. Ten minutes or so later she was seated in The Laurels's dining room, savoring fish pie and sipping San Pellegrino. The pie was good, and under normal circumstances would have merited a glass of decent white wine or a good draught beer, either of which the Laurels was evidently well equipped to provide. But Cecilia the police officer was cautious of driving with even a trace of alcohol on her breath, and so virtuously restrained her gastronomic instincts.

"May I join you?"

She looked up to see a middle aged, cheerful looking woman

wearing a clerical collar and a wonderfully colored smock that looked vaguely middle-eastern.

"Susanna!" she said. "Yes, of course—please do. What a nice surprise!"

Susanna Metz was an American priest who'd come into the diocese of Exeter at about the same time as Michael. He had on several occasions after especially tedious diocesan meetings brought Susanna back to the vicarage for tea, cake, and mutual debriefing, and so Cecilia had met her and enjoyed her company.

Susanna was Vicar of Petrockstowe and also, Cecilia gathered—the church suffering at present from a shortage of both priests and money—of just about every other church in the vicinity. After a few minutes several other people joined them—parishioners, she gathered, and most of them farmers. Susanna introduced her, and the conversation became general.

"So what does everyone think about U.N.I.T.E.D. coming to Edgestow?" Cecilia asked when there seemed to be a suitable moment.

"Government chap on the radio the other day said it's going to put north Devon on the map," one of them said. "My problem is, I'm actually pretty happy being *off* the map."

Several of them nodded and one or two laughed.

"Have you seen the place?" one of them asked her.

"No, not yet," she said.

"It's huge—all glass and steel and skyscrapery. Weird. Gives me the creeps just to look at it, and it doesn't really fit round here at all."

"Of course," another put in, "there are some good things about it. It's created a few jobs."

"Not as many as you'd think, though," a woman said. "The big firms doing the major buildings and constructing the motorway mostly bring in their own people from outside. There's not been all that much in it for our folk. Sometimes it feels almost like they're trying to keep us out. And it isn't just that it's costing us jobs, it's, well, odd."

"Though I've heard that chap who's been put in charge of it—what's his name? Sir James something?'

"Harlow," someone said.

"Harlow, that's right—well, I hear he's been raising a bit of a stink about that. Says they've *got* to employ more people from round here if they want the contracts. So maybe things will get better."

"Perhaps they will. Saw him on TV. He seems all right. And at least he's a Devon man—even if not quite from the best part!"

There was a general chuckle. The Harlow's historic family seat was near Paignton, in the southern part of the county. Naturally those of more northern stock held themselves to be superior.

"There was a big international institute in Edgestow in the 1940s, wasn't there?" Cecilia said. "The National Institute for Co-ordinated Experiments?"

"That's right—N.I.C.E.," an older man said. "And it came to a very sticky end. Not just the earthquake, I mean after that. There was a public inquiry and it came out they'd been up to some very dirty business."

"I think," Susanna said, "and stop me if I'm wrong, that what happened back then is one of the things that's giving people bad vibes about what's happening now."

"That's right," the older man said, "I remember my dad going on about how the N.I.C.E. police used to throw their weight about. Dead narked he'd be, just remembering it. Well, now the new lot has brought in some funny people to do its security, too. Latvians, they are. For the life of me I can't see why they couldn't find somebody British to do it. Half of them don't seem able to speak English. And when they're on site they're armed to the teeth, apparently. Doesn't seem right."

"Where you've got a lot of guns swilling about, somebody's going to get hurt," the man next to him said. "Stands to reason."

Cecilia nodded in a way she hoped was noncommittal. She was here to calm fears, but far be it from her to discourage an Englishman's common-sense aversion to the presence of unnecessary firearms.

"To be fair," the man went on, "I'm pretty sure most of them are decent enough lads. The only one I've talked to came to church on Sunday, and he was just keen to earn enough money at the security job here so he could get back home and marry his girl."

"I dare say most of them are all right," the older man said, "but there's certainly one or two of them who've been carrying on like they think they're the Gestapo. And of course after a few pints some of our lads can get a bit antsy too. There've been a couple of punch-ups. Police had to come out from Exeter last time."

He turned to Cecilia.

"But I dare say you know about that and that's why you're here."

Cecilia nodded. It was no secret, and the chief constable and Sir James Harlow had, after all, given that interview on television.

"Pretty much, yes," she said.

Needless to say, as a result of all this conversation, lunch took a good deal longer than Cecilia had planned. But that was fine by her. She departed from the Laurels dining room and Susanna's parishioners not only replete with fish pie and usefully informed as to how at least some local people perceived her presence and the presence of U.N.I.T.E.D. but also — and rather pleasantly — feeling a good deal more at home in north Devon.

Susanna walked with her back to the car. For a moment they enjoyed a companionable silence.

"Well, I need to go and milk the cows," Susanna said, "my girls, as I generally call them!" She smiled. "It's one of the things

I get to do, besides being parish priest. Give my best to Michael, will you?"

"Of course."

The priest paused for moment longer, seeming to feel for words.

"You know, I've come to love this place. One of the fields where I get to help with the cows is on top of a hill. On a clear day you can see for miles across to the other farms and south right on toward the hills of Dartmoor. Sometimes the wind gets blustery and every bit of nature's 'charged with grandeur,' as Hopkins puts it. Then it's time to go back and I get to feel nothing could be more beautiful than walking home on a cold evening with cows—feeling their breath warm on your back and hearing them snort with interest at things they've found to chomp in the hedgerows."

"I believe you," Cecilia said.

"The thing is, though—it's a wonderful way of life, and all this"—Susanna gestured at what was around them, the village green, the pub, the church, the cross of Saint George fluttering above them—"it's precious. But it's vulnerable, I think. Threatened. And especially right now. Try to take care of it for us, will you? Some of our people here are very nervous about these new high-powered developments and what they may do to us—not just U.N.I.T.E.D., though that's what they're focused on at the moment—but the agribusinesses and all that. And to tell you the truth, so am I."

Cecilia nodded.

"We'll do our best," she said.

EIGHT

West of Petrockstowe.

Leaving Petrockstowe, Cecilia followed for several miles a winding road between high hedges—mostly beech, she thought—up to the village of St. Anne's-on-the-Hill, where she passed a stone cross, another seventeenth-century pub, and another medieval church (was Susanna vicar of this one, too?). From Saint Anne's the road led her gently down again between more hedges, occasional gaps on either side revealing a rolling patchwork of fields, some green, some gold, some red Devon earth. At one point she had to stop for several minutes while two young women in stained blue coveralls and muddy wellingtons brought a herd of mixed cows across the road: among them, somewhat to her surprise, two bulls, who appeared, however, to walk docilely enough among the females.

She wondered what would happen if one of the cows—or, worse, one of the bulls—became obstreperous. Someone had pointed out to her only recently that farming, contrary to popular imagery, was a dangerous occupation. Still, the young women seemed calm enough, and they and their charges passed into the field without incident.

She drove on.

Soon there was a handsome stone wall to her left, interrupted at one point by an equally handsome wooden double door, with a wicket gate and a painted wooden notice beside it, white lettering on blue, "Saint Boniface Abbey." Then more hedges for about another mile, until at last she came face to face with a large road sign, "Welcome to Edgestow."

At once the road straightened out and became wider, as if deciding that it was now part of a town and so ought to be more businesslike. This was still the older part of Edgestow, the part that had survived the 1945 earthquake. It consisted mostly of 1930's houses, with a few postwar creations among them. There was a Spar supermarket and a nice-looking pub, The Great Western. The branch line that served Saint Anne's had of course been closed for years, but the brightly painted sign still showed a locomotive in the livery of the old Great Western Railway, with clouds of white steam billowing cheerfully from its brass-rimmed chimney.

Cecilia smiled, and drove on until the land — and therefore the road following it — suddenly fell away. She found herself looking down into a shallow valley that had once contained the old town of Edgestow and its university, but was now home to U.N.I.T.E.D.

She brought the car to a halt, got out so that she could see better, and whistled softly.

It was certainly impressive — there was no denying that. An array of buildings a mile or so across, all dark reflective glass and shining metal. In the center a tower, also shining glass and metal, stretched tall and stark toward the sky. To her left the new motorway curved in from the west. The waters of the River Wynd gleamed softly in the foreground. In the 1940s there had, she gathered, been attempts to divert it, but the earthquake had put an end to all that, and after briefly flooding the valley the river had returned to what was more or less its original course.

Cecilia could hardly believe what she was seeing. U.N.I.T.E.D. was much bigger than she'd expected.

"That's not what I'd call an institute," she muttered. "It's a city. A city and a tower."

And it must utterly, violently have changed the landscape. She looked up at the hills and fields beyond, with clouds rolling in from the sea. Then she looked back at the glass and metal of U.N.I.T.E.D.

No wonder it made Susanna and some of the local people nervous. And the man in the Laurels who'd described it for her had been right. The institute sat there, all glass and steel and skyscrapery. And it didn't fit.

She surveyed the scene for a several more minutes, then got back into the car, turned it around, and drove back through the older part of Edgestow.

To get to the temporary police station she knew she needed to turn off from the road she'd come in by, but she didn't know precisely where. She *could* stop the car and program the satnav. Instead, she pulled over to the side, lowered the window, and asked a young woman who was walking by with a baby in a pram. For her trouble she received a bright smile and good directions, and found what she was looking for without difficulty: two very large trailers parked in the gardens of what had once been a small private hotel and would soon be converted into the new Edgestow Police Station.

There Sergeant Wyatt welcomed her, already at his usual position behind the front desk.

"It's good to see you, Sergeant," she said. "Everything else looks a bit strange."

"We'll soon have it all ticking over, ma'am."

"Any problems so far?"

"Biggest drama today, ma'am, has been a lady who'd lost her marmalade cat around nine o'clock and came in to tell me all about it midmorning. Just about the time she's finished telling me, in rushes a little girl. Apparently she's the little girl from the house next door but one, and she tells us the marmalade cat's turned up and her mama's giving him a saucer of milk to keep him occupied. So the lady went off rejoicing, and I closed the case."

"Excellent, Sergeant. That's just the kind of police work I like."

NINE

"Some elements in the order of precedence are clear," Michael said, "even after a mere thirty-six hours. For example, it's obvious that your mama and Rachel outrank Papa and me. Figaro outranks Tocco and Pu, who constitute his canine army: theirs not to reason why, theirs but to do and — well, generally make a rumpus if so ordered. Felix and Marlene of course continue to occupy their own parallel universe in which cats in general and they in particular are the all-wise and all-powerful rulers. I must admit, though, when I think about your mama and Rachel, I'm not at all sure who's in charge. Mama clearly thinks she is, but I don't think Rachel does, and it certainly doesn't always look like that. What I *am* sure of is that your papa and I come at the bottom of *all* lists. We'll be here for the next twelve weeks to do as we're told, take our share of cooking, walk dogs, feed dogs *and* cats, and occasionally make ourselves useful if heavy lifting's needed. Our opinion *may* at times be sought on some matter of national importance such as where Rachel left her teddy bear. Otherwise we'll be pretty well free to get on with our own little affairs, such as Andrea's seminars or the parish, just so long as they don't interfere with the grownups."

Cecilia, who'd been giggling throughout this monologue, laughed. They were talking on her mini iPad. Michael's tone was light and he looked happy. Evidently things were going well.

And evidently she-who-would-one-day-rule-the galaxy had recovered her spirits.

"And by the way," he said, "Mama's looking after your plants."

"A good thing, too," she said. Her husband's deficiencies in this respect had become apparent some months ago when she returned from a weekend conference to find several of her favorites drooping and disconsolate. She had not been amused.

"So how are your digs?" he said. "The B&B? What's it like?"

"Actually it's very nice. It's a small flat, really, and I've even got my own front door."

"And is your landlady all right?"

Cecilia laughed.

"I should say so! I have to admit, I think Mrs. Abney was a bit taken aback when I turned up. They'd booked the place for me and given her my name over the phone. As a result she thought her guest was going to be a Detective Chief Inspector *Carver*, and I think she expected him to be like John Barnaby in 'Midsomer Murders.' So when what showed up was me, a female with a funny name, she had something of a shock. But then when she came into the flat later to give me the keys and saw the photo of you in your clerical collar with Rachel and I told her who you both were, I think she decided I might be all right. And now after chatting with her at breakfast I think she's actually getting quite turned on to the idea of playing host to an Italian lady policeman who's married to a vicar! You and Rachel are already invited to come and stay here whenever you like."

"Good heavens, an assignation! We'll definitely come."

"Wait a minute, you haven't heard the best of it yet. Of course when they booked the place they told her I might be working weird hours—but the deal is, if I'm here in the morning and stick my head round her kitchen door between six and seven, I get breakfast. *And she really can cook!* She makes her own bread—and the smell of that wafting into the bedroom at about five-forty is alone enough to make you think it's worth getting up—and she makes coffee that tastes like coffee. And as for her traditional English breakfast—I'll just say it's highly likely your personal Italian lady policeman will return to you several kilos heavier than when she left! So now do you still want to come?"

"Absolutely!" he said.

A pause.

"And what about Edgestow generally?" he said.

"Ugly, modern, and huge as far as the institute is concerned, but pleasant enough as regards the rest. And the rest is all that matters to us, really. If today is anything to go by, policing the town really shouldn't be too difficult. To tell you the truth, after all the fuss I made about not wanting to come here, I feel somewhat embarrassed. The people I've met all seem to be nice, and it occurs to me that there must be something really rather wonderful about a community where so little that was criminal happened between 1945 and 2013 that they were able to manage with only one police officer."

She paused for a moment.

"I think," she added, "that the important thing for us will be simply to make sure that we're visible. Let people see friendly uniforms and panda cars about. In the town Chief Superintendent Davies suggested having some old-fashioned foot patrols, and Sergeant Wyatt and I have tried to pick PCs who'll be good at that."

She paused again.

"Mind you," she said, "I can see why U.N.I.T.E.D. is making some of the local people edgy. It's not only ugly. It's colossal—out of all proportion to everything round it. So far I've only seen it from the top of the hill, but it's virtually a city, all glass and metal with a great skyscrapery tower in the middle. A city and a tower. Isn't there something like that in the Bible? A vision of the New Jerusalem or something?"

Michael chuckled.

"There's certainly something like that in the Bible—but it's hardly the New Jerusalem."

"What is it then?"

"It's the Tower of Babel," he said.

TEN

Edgestow. 7:30 a.m. Thursday, 29th August 2013

When Cecilia arrived at the temporary station the next morning, Sergeant Wyatt was waiting for her with a message.

"Ma'am, the chief super's been on the phone and he'd like you to call him as soon as you get in."

So she did.

"Good morning, Detective *Chief* Inspector Cavaliere," Davies said. "All's well, I trust?"

"I think so, sir. So far, anyway."

"Good. Well there are two things you need to know about. First, there's a possible situation I want you to look into. Did you hear about the multi-car pile-up on the A30 last Thursday?"

"I saw it on the news, sir."

"Overall," he said, "of course it's one for RCIT."

By which he meant the Road Crash Investigation Team, generally known among her colleagues as *ass-sit*.

"*Except*," he continued, "that they've found two bodies in a van that was part of the pile-up, sealed into a hidden compartment. Illegals. Nigerians, by the papers and letters in their wallets. Whoever was driving must have panicked after the crash and done a bunk—leaving them to die, as it turns out. Forensics says they have to have been alive for several hours, during which time they could have been treated if anyone had known they were there. They bled to death. Not pretty."

"No sir."

"Well, they traced the van. It belongs to a Charles Frasier in London. Small business. Electronics, TVs, that sort of thing. Uses it for delivery. No convictions. Nothing known against him. So far as we can see, a law-abiding, tax-paying citizen. *He* says he'd lent the van for the weekend to his brother, William Frasier, who'd had a chance to earn some money delivering second-hand furniture from France, but no wheels. William took the van on Wednesday and since then Charles heard nothing until the Met came to the door. He claims he knows nothing at all about any hidden compartments, and maybe he doesn't. The work on them looks new and could have been added for this trip. We do know a bit about brother William, though. Nasty piece of work. Petty theft, mostly, but a string of convictions—which I suppose means he isn't particularly good at it! British and French customs confirm he took the van over from Newhaven to Dieppe on Wednesday afternoon and came back with it by the same route on Thursday morning. Later the same day, ANPR cameras picked up the van at various points on the roads between Newhaven and Honiton."

Cecilia nodded. Automatic Number Plate Recognition, established in Britain since 2006 and linked to the Police National Computer, was an invaluable way of keeping track of vehicles the police were interested in.

"Then finally," Davies said, "it was involved in that crash on the A30 just past Honiton on Thursday afternoon."

"Do they actually know for sure that it was still William Frasier driving the van when it crashed?"

It wasn't her case, but she couldn't stop herself from asking the question. What we can't show, we don't know.

"Well, yes, I think they do, pretty well. Thanks to all those convictions, we have William Frasier's DNA and fingerprints on file, and according to RCIT they're all over the van—steering wheel, door handles, packet of cigarettes, cigarette butts, greasy wrappings from a MacDonald's cheeseburger—"

Cecilia shuddered, but said nothing.

"—dirty paper napkins, you name it! He's obviously a messy fellow, to say the least. And there's no sign of anyone else being there, so far as they can see, except a few prints here and there which turn out to be from the brother, as you'd expect. But William Frasier's prints seem to overlay all the others—especially those on the steering wheel and the doors. So yes, I think we can be pretty sure he was driving when the van crashed."

Cecilia nodded. That sounded reasonable enough.

"They did find some ruts and footprints on a grassy bank near the crashed van," Davies continued. "It looks as if someone climbed up it, and then after that worked his way along the side of a field to the road. Presumably that was William Frasier too, though I admit they can't be quite so sure of that. They're checking the surrounding area now, pubs and so on, but so far no word of anyone being seen or turning up anywhere who might be him."

Cecilia waited.

Fascinating though this all was, it was hard to see what it had to do with her. But doubtless the chief superintendent would get there in the end. He was a good man (Welsh, like her friend DS Verity Jones) but not generally known for brevity (nor was Verity, as it happened).

"So much for tracing the driver. But there is one other thing. One other lead they found when they were taking the van apart yesterday morning—which was later than it should have been, but they've been swamped with stuff, not least from that pile-up."

Ah, perhaps this would turn out to be the point.

"Between the seats—it must have been catapulted there when the van spun around—was a TomTom satellite navigation system. It had been programmed to give directions, and the destination was your Edgestow institute, I'm afraid. The United Nations Institute for Technological Experimentation and Development."

"U.N.I.T.E.D.? How extraordinary! What on earth would they have to do with illegal immigrants?"

"A good question! So that's the reason I'm calling you. I don't really think the U.N. is on a scam to get illegal immigrants into the United Kingdom, but I suppose someone working for them might be. In any case the van does seem to have been heading to their institute and we need to check it out."

"I'm on it, sir."

"Good. Now, change of subject! The second thing you need to know about is this. There's a general terrorist advisement out from MI5. Nothing specific. Just information they've received that someone's going to try something on the British mainland in the next few days. Not Al Qaeda or anything like that. They seem to think it might be that Teflon fellow again."

"I'm sorry sir, I'm obviously not as well up with major crime as I should be. Who's Teflon?"

"Well, the fact is no one knows who he is—we don't even know for sure it's a 'he.' So far there's no name, no nationality, nothing. I suppose that's why they call him—or her—Teflon. Nothing ever sticks. But they do know what he does. He robs banks, buys arms with the proceeds, provides the arms to fighters in Africa in exchange for diamonds, then sells the diamonds in Europe or the United States for a colossal profit."

"Neophyte question, sir—but why not just rob the banks and buy the diamonds?"

"Because the people they're dealing with don't want money— they want weapons. And before you ask, the amount they get for the diamonds in western markets will always be far greater than what they have to pay for the weapons."

"Is that what they call 'blood diamonds'?"

"That's right."

Cecilia nodded. She'd heard of "blood diamonds, or "conflict diamonds" as they were sometimes called. Over the last ten years there had been serious international efforts to stop the trade, and they'd had some success, but it was by no means totally shut down.

The chief superintendent, of course, had more to tell her.

"This Teflon fellow's pulled off three massive thefts so far — one in New York, one in Milan, and one in Stockholm. What's interesting is his MO. He starts by causing a major disruption the night before that has police and emergency services running all over the place. In New York it was a subway breakdown in the rush hour — chaos with thousands of commuters stranded. In Milan and Stockholm he managed to knock out all the traffic lights in the rush hour. Similar result. Then at some point the following morning, while everyone's still trying to recover from the previous evening's adventures, he organizes something even more dramatic. In New York a place called the Hogan warehouse in downtown Manhattan caught fire. In Milan a car exploded in a schoolyard and killed a lot of kids. In Stockholm he blew up three cars more or less simultaneously in adjacent streets. Then while the already stretched police and emergency services were trying to cope with all that, his people went in and robbed two or three local banks. So far it's worked like a charm. Since he obviously likes major cities, I hardly think Devon's going to figure particularly high on his list of possible targets. Still, you never know. We do have a cathedral city and we do have some banks and securities firms, so I pass the advisement to you for what it's worth. Of course I'll fax you all the details."

"Yes, sir. It does seem odd, though."

"Odd?"

"Yes — I mean, we've got all this information about how Teflon operates and even why — and yet we don't even know if we're looking for a man or a woman. I not sure it quite adds up. I wonder where MI5 got this information?"

"The word on the street is it's from the Americans."

"Oh." A pause. "And we think they're trustworthy?"

"About as trustworthy as we are."

She chuckled.

"Fair enough."

"At least, I think they're as anxious as anyone to see this fellow put out of business. Anyway, it's the usual drill. Tell your people to be on the lookout for anything unusual or suspicious, and if they see it, report it fast. All right?"

"Yes sir. I'll see that everyone's told."

ELEVEN

Edgestow, the temporary police station. 8:20 a.m.

Cecilia passed on the terror advisement to her officers.

"Bloody Muslims," one of the PCs muttered.

"Constable," she said, "there are one point two billion Muslims in the world and ninety-nine point nine recurring per cent of them want to live in peace. What's more, over two point seven million of them are *your* fellow citizens whom *you* are employed to serve and protect. So if ever I hear you make a bigoted remark like that again, I'll report you — and I don't think you'll like the repercussions."

The offender was young, doubtless simply echoing prejudices he'd heard from others. He had the grace to look ashamed.

"Sorry, ma'am."

She nodded. "Anyway, as you'll have gathered if you've been paying any attention at all to what I've just been saying, according to our information this particular terrorist threat doesn't have anything to do with religion. Just plain old-fashioned greed, a phenomenon from which you may have noticed even some Christians and agnostics are not entirely free."

Several of them grinned.

"Yes, ma'am."

"We get it, ma'am."

She took DS Verity Jones with her to visit U.N.I.T.E.D.

Verity, immaculate as usual and cheerfully elfin today in her green and yellow trouser suit, was a pleasing contrast to the morning, which was mild but overcast.

"The weather forecast said it was going to be sunny," Verity said.

"Papà says the trouble with the English weather forecast is you can't even guarantee it's going to be wrong."

They drove down into the Edgestow valley, past various lots and building sites, over the River Wynd by the new bridge, and so came to the institute, at whose entrance a swing barrier blocked the road. It was supervised from an adjacent glass fronted kiosk.

Cecilia and Verity produced their warrant cards and identified themselves. Cecilia indicated they needed to speak to someone in authority. The barrier was raised and they were directed, as she had expected, toward the central tower.

As they drove through the complex, she found it on closer inspection rather less impressive than it had seemed at first sight from the hill. Many of the buildings were unfinished. Others looked to be empty. At one point they passed a dozen or so articulated lorries, which had presumably come in by the new motorway and were now parked irregularly alongside the road to the tower. There was a great deal of scurrying about and shouting by men in coveralls and hard hats, and a lot of heavy machinery roaring and clattering, but the work did not seem to be all that well organized. Parts of the road surface were excellent. Others were rutted and uneven, and Verity had to steer round potholes. And almost everywhere Cecilia looked there were security guards—young men in dark gray uniforms with "Eglītis" stitched in bright yellow letters on the breast pocket.

Most of them were toting Heckler and Koch MP5s, just as the chief super had said they'd be. It all felt very un-English. And to her at least, unappealing.

About halfway to their destination, she suddenly had the extraordinary feeling of being lifted: for an instant not just she herself but the car, the road, everything seemed to have reared out of place, to be suspended in air, in the wrong space. She watched as Verity quickly but coolly brought the car to a halt and took it out of drive—and yet quick though she was, by the time she had done so, whatever had happened was already over.

There was a moment of silence, of stillness.

Someone started up a piece of machinery.

One of the men in gray uniforms shouted something in a foreign language—Latvian, Cecilia assumed—to another man, who shouted back.

And everything went back to the way it was.

"What on earth was that?" she said.

"It was an earth tremor, ma'am. I've experienced them once or twice in Wales. They seldom do much harm in Britain. Maybe crack the odd window."

"Oh. Well I haven't experienced one before, or at least not to notice. It's unnerving, isn't it?"

"It is, ma'am. Apparently they've had quite a few of them round here over the last week or so."

"But the experts all say the place is safe now, don't they?"

"That's what they *say*," Verity replied as she slid the automatic back into drive.

TWELVE

The center of the U.N.I.T.E.D. complex, a few minutes later

They approached the glass and steel tower, its sheer sides gleaming darkly beneath the gray morning sky. A shining wine-colored Daimler DS 420 limousine was parked in front of the high glass and chrome entrance doors.

"*Serious* money!" Verity said, nodding towards the magnificent car as she drove past it, made a U-turn, and then brought their Ford Fiesta to a stop behind it.

Cecilia smiled to herself. The last time she'd heard anyone use that expression was when she and Michael were leaving a restaurant in London during their first weeks together. A passerby had said it about her dress, a natty little number that she and mama had bought for her a few days previously at the Oxfam shop.

"Could it be they have visiting royals?" Verity said.

"I doubt there'd be royals here without someone bothering to tell us," Cecilia said. "My money is on a wealthy tycoon. Maybe an oil-rich sheik."

But as they got out of their car, Sir James Harlow emerged from the glass double-doors to the tower, accompanied by two young men in dark suits who were carrying briefcases.

Cecilia thought he looked tired, but his face lit up and he smiled broadly when he saw her.

"Cecilia!" he said, "Detective *Chief* Inspector Cavaliere! What a pleasant surprise!"

He nodded to the young men to go ahead of him to the Daimler, then turned back to her.

"The chief constable told me about your promotion, Cecilia, and that you'll be in charge down here for a bit. I'm delighted. I was intending to drop you a line congratulating you. From all that I hear from your colleagues, they couldn't have picked anyone better. Edgestow is lucky to have you."

"Thank you, sir."

"And is Father Michael well?"

"Yes sir—or he was yesterday evening when we talked."

"Excellent. Please do give him my very best regards when you talk with him again, will you? And this lady, I take it, is your colleague?"

Cecilia introduced Verity.

"I'm delighted to meet you, Detective Sergeant Jones. It's good to know that the Queen's peace in Edgestow is in such obviously capable hands. But there, I'm sure you two didn't come all the way out here just to hear an old man rattling on. Is there something you need from us? Can U.N.I.T.E.D. be of assistance to you in some way?"

Briefly, Cecilia told Sir James about the A30 pile-up, the overturned van with no driver, the bodies of the illegal immigrants, and, of course, about U.N.I.T.E.D.'s address found programmed into the van's GPS navigation system.

"How utterly terrible and how extraordinary!" Sir James said when she finished. "Well, we must certainly follow up on all that. Look, I have to be away from here for the next forty-eight hours—the government has some kind of diplomatic thing in Paris they want me to look into. Otherwise I'd be happy to stay and try to help you myself. But if you go to the main desk in the atrium and tell them who you are, they'll get you with Louis

Cartwright straightaway. He's my deputy, and he'll do all he can. I trust it goes without saying that we'll want to cooperate fully with any inquiry."

After polite leave-taking, Sir James joined his colleagues in the Daimler. It pulled away, silently and swiftly, as Cecilia and Verity entered the U.N.I.T.E.D. tower.

THIRTEEN

The U.N.I.T.E.D. tower, a few minutes later.

O nce they were inside the atrium, the noise and somewhat frenetic busyness that had marked their drive across the outer complex might never have been. They entered another world: a world of calm, silence, and soft carpets. There were handsome sofas and armchairs, indoor plants, even a fountain. Actually, the atrium was not quite silent: in the background, good quality speakers were softly playing *Eine Kleine Nachtmusik*. The place reminded Cecilia somewhat of Cranston College in East London—a recollection that gave her mixed feelings. On the one hand, Cranston College was the first place she'd ever gone to alone with Michael, and although the occasion had hardly been an *appuntamento amoroso*, she rather thought that was the evening when it first began to dawn on her how very much she liked him. On the other hand, Cranston College was where they had encountered a monstrous evil that had threatened to destroy them and a great deal more besides.

She sighed and shook her head. That was all in the past now, thank God—all except Michael, and he, thank God, was still very much a part of her present.

An enormous marble-topped reception desk stood at the center of the atrium and there, as Sir James had suggested, she identified herself and Verity to a tall young man who nodded politely and made a call. She smiled to see that around his telephone were several brightly colored plastic ducks.

"We're all a bit serious here," he said, noting her smile. "I thought the place could do with a bit of cheering up."

After a brief interval a man in his thirties appeared: dark business suit, dark blue shirt, and silver tie with a Windsor knot.

"Good morning," Cecilia said, as she and Verity yet again produced their warrant cards. "I'm Detective Chief Inspector Cecilia Cavaliere of Exeter CID. This is my colleague Detective Sergeant Verity Jones."

"Good morning to you both."

An American accent—from the midwest, she thought, although identifying American accents wasn't her strongest suit.

"I'm Herbert Grieg," he said, "and I'm assistant to the director of the institute. I'm sorry Sir James isn't here today. The foreign office is whipping him off to Paris for highly secret negotiations—the word on the street is they're about Syria. But who knows? Anyway, Mr. Cartwright, our deputy director, *is* here and he'll be happy to see you. He's using the director's office. Please, follow me. We'll have to take the elevator, as the director's office is on the twentieth floor. In some ways it's not convenient, but I promise you the views are simply fantastic. You'll see."

The lift was swift and silent, and one might not have realized it was moving at all were it not for a soft "click" as they passed the floors. They stopped at the fifteenth and eighteenth to let various staff members on and off, then just the three of them ascended from the eighteenth to the twentieth. For this part of the ascent, there was one more click than Cecilia expected. She glanced at Verity, but said nothing.

FOURTEEN

*Edgestow, the U.N.I.T.E.D. tower. The director's office.
A minute or so later.*

The director's office was full of light, and the views from its wide windows were indeed stunning: north Devon hedgerows and fields in three directions and in a fourth—beyond the fields and hedgerows, misty with distance—the tors and wilderness of Dartmoor.

Cecilia stood enthralled by this—for her, at any rate—unusual view of the ancient landscape. She and Michael had walked and picnicked on Dartmoor several times, and intended to take Rachel as soon as she was big enough. Some people found the moor's wildness and bleakness threatening. They loved it. In a way she thought that the ancients had misnamed it—*mór*, "dead land," if that indeed was what the Old English word meant—for it seemed to her that the moor was anything but dead. Rather, she found it full of life. And strong. But it had never been tamed. Its life and its strength were its own. It demanded respect, and if you didn't give it respect it could and would play tricks on you, dangerous tricks, even fatal tricks if you were foolish enough to ignore its warnings. The moor was a reminder that Britain—even Europe—had not always been civilized and safe. It had once been a land of dark forests and small kingdoms, of mists and marshes and the threat of enchantments, and it could be those things still, if —

She heard her name and realized that the deputy director was welcoming them — a large, balding man who had risen to his feet at their entrance and now stood beaming at them from behind a big desk: English public school accent, knitted tie, Harris Tweed jacket and waistcoat.

"... and Detective Sergeant Jones as well. I'm afraid that Sir James is away from us today, as I believe my colleague Mr. Grieg has told you. He is gone forth from us into the world to perform mighty works!"

"We met Sir James at the entrance, sir," Cecilia said.

"Ah, excellent! Well, I am Louis Cartwright, his deputy, and I will do my very best to be a substitute. Please, ladies, be seated! May I offer you some refreshment? A coffee, perhaps? Or tea?"

They sat but politely declined the coffee or tea.

"Well then, Detective Chief Inspector, how can we help you?"

Herbert Grieg withdrew discreetly to a smaller desk in the corner and appeared to busy himself with papers.

Cecilia again told the story of the crash, the driverless van, the bodies of the two illegal immigrants — evidently from Africa — and the satellite navigation system programmed to give directions to the U.N. institute.

"As I'm sure you'll appreciate, sir, it's not just a matter of illegal immigration. It's almost certainly a matter of criminal manslaughter, possibly murder. These men needn't have died. Someone left them there to bleed to death. We want to know who, and why. And in connection with all that, we'd like to know how the address of the institute came to be in the van's satellite navigation system, so we need to ask whether you or anyone else here can cast any light on that."

Cartwright looked astonished.

"How extraordinary! And how terrible! I honestly have no

way to account for any of this. Have you any thoughts, Mr. Grieg?"

The assistant to the director shook his head.

"Believe me," Cartwright said, "I would help you if I could. You say the driver just left those poor fellows to bleed to death?"

"It certainly looks like it, sir."

"That is a terrible, shameful story. You know, we work here in a place like this for peace, for progress for the human race. We are developing some of the most sophisticated scenarios ever envisaged—for biology, for the climate, for the evolution of humanity. We are building computers that will be capable of removing much of the uncertainty and pain of human life, of creating something like paradise. And then something like this happens that suggests we aren't far removed from barbarians. Is fallen humanity capable of paradise?"

"I don't know, sir. But I do know we've got two people dead, and some connection to this organization. Do you think there's any place in the institute where illegal immigrants might be being employed? In the kitchens? On the building sites?"

"Detective Chief Inspector, I am sure I speak for Sir James as well as myself when I say that you're welcome to check anywhere on the site, and all our dining facilities. And you're welcome to check everyone employed here, beginning with myself. If there are undocumented workers in the institute, it is certainly unknown to me, and to my assistants—and against our wishes." He glanced at Grieg, who nodded his agreement. "So please, feel free to go anywhere you will in the institute and talk to anyone you like."

"That's most helpful of you, sir."

"Well, we just want to cooperate in any way we can."

He seemed to ruminate.

"Of course it may be that we were the intended *target* of some criminal activity. There is a great deal of equipment in this complex, all of it very advanced, and much of it immensely valuable. Herbert,"—he looked towards his assistant—"is working with some of it. Perhaps the intention was, as I believe criminals put it, to 'case the joint.' Perhaps that's why the van was coming here."

Thereby gently indicating, Cecilia reflected, that the connection between the van and the institute was entirely circumstantial.

Cartwright, however, seemed to have decided that a touch of righteous indignation was now called for.

"Frankly, it makes me angry just to think of those poor fellows coming all the way here from Nigeria—hoping to make new lives for themselves I suppose—and then being left like that to bleed to death. It's horrific, and I'll do anything I can to help bring the perpetrators to book."

Cecilia rose to her feet before he could continue.

"Well, that's very good of you, sir," she said. "And I'll certainly notify my superiors of everything you've said." She glanced at Verity. "I think, Mr. Cartwright, that for the moment we've done what we can. So I'll bid you good morning."

"And good morning to you, Detective Chief Inspector Cavaliere. Detective Sergeant Jones! It's been a great pleasure to meet you both. As I am sure you know, my good friend and colleague Sir James Harlow is most anxious that the closest and most amicable of relationships be maintained between those of us here at the institute and those generally responsible for maintaining law and order in Edgestow. This, I hope, has been a good beginning. Herbert, would you very kindly show our guests down to the entrance?" A deprecating smile.

"No, Mr. Deputy Director." Herbert Grieg pressed a button on his desk and rose to his feet. "I very kindly will *not* do that."

As he spoke, the door beside him opened, and three young men entered the office. They were wearing the dark gray uniforms and the yellow "Eglītis" of the institute's internal security, and they were carrying MP5s.

"Herbert!" the deputy director said. "What on earth are you doing?"

"I'm doing what's necessary," his assistant said. "You damn fool, can't you see they've rumbled you?"

FIFTEEN

The same, a few minutes later

Herbert Grieg was right.

Cecilia had indeed rumbled the deputy director, and it was clear to her that Verity had too. Apparently the deputy director was the only one who didn't get it.

"Herbert, what on earth are you talking about?" Cartwright said. "Are you mad? How have they 'rumbled' us?"

"Not *us*, asshole! *You*! Because the boss police lady here left out one detail in her narrative and you, perfect English gentleman that you are, very kindly supplied it. She said the immigrants in the truck were from Africa. Nobody mentioned Nigeria — *until you did!*"

Cartwright looked crestfallen as Grieg dismissed him with a wave of the hand and turned back to Cecilia and Verity.

"Now hear this, ladies. The little plan I'm sure you had of getting a search warrant and then coming back with half the Brit police force isn't going to work. And as of this moment I'm telling my colleagues here, my Latvian friends, to kill you both if I have the slightest trouble with either of you. Your lives hang by a thread, and the thread is this — alive, you just might be useful to me in a little project I'm working on."

He gazed at them for a moment.

"Actually, he said, "it isn't little, it's big, bigger than anything either of you has ever been involved in or seen in your whole lives. But big or little, I was managing it *before* you arrived and I can go on managing it if you disappear. Is that clear?"

"Yes," Cecilia said quietly.

The situation was out of her control, and Grieg had, in fact, described her planned reaction to Cartwright's slip pretty well. For the moment the thing was to stay calm, alert, and of course, alive. The three young men looked like professionals, and she certainly didn't intend to test the sincerity of Grieg's warning. She glanced at Verity, who merely shrugged.

"Good," Grieg said. "Now, one of these fine young men is going to search you, each in turn. What we want, of course, are cell phones, weapons, anything else you could use to cause us trouble. Ozols, you can do that. The boss lady first," he said, pointing to Cecilia. "Our friends Balodis and Pētersons will keep you both covered while this is going on, and if *you*" — to Cecilia — "try to use some clever judo trick or other on Ozols while you're at close quarters, the first thing you'll discover is that Ozols is pretty good at judo too, and the second is that Balodis and Pētersons will have killed your sidekick. Is that clear?"

Cecilia nodded.

"Perfectly clear," she said.

"I dare say you'll disapprove of our not having females available to search females, but if your people will insist on sending women to do a man's job, what can they expect? Get on with it, Ozols."

To be fair to Ozols, he took no advantage of the situation. The result of his work was two mobile telephones from Cecilia and one from Verity.

"I hate to waste good electronics, but…"

Grieg walked over to his desk, took out a small hammer from the drawer, and with a few swift blows shattered the three phones.

"What about their car, Mr. Grieg? It is parked at our entrance."

The security guard's voice was thickly accented.

"Good thought, Balodis. Is it a police car?"

"It is not marked as a police car. A plain blue Ford. A Fiesta."

"Well, we must get it out of sight and off the premises anyway. Is the big transporter truck still here?"

"Yes, Mr. Grieg."

"Okay. Drive it up into that, and then take it somewhere pretty far from civilization, or what passes for civilization around here, and hide it."

He gestured toward the window and the Devon countryside beyond it.

"Cover it with branches or earth, whatever it takes. And make sure whoever handles it wears gloves. Presumably the police will find it sooner or later and we don't want anything in it connecting to anyone here. Hold it on the ramp when you're putting it into the transporter. And hose it down—hose the underneath, too. It could have picked up some of our dirt from going over all those damned potholes."

"Maybe there is a tracking device on their car, Mr. Grieg."

"It'll surely have a radio. Just make sure it's turned off. I doubt there's a transponder, but you can check. Don't take too long about it, though. Sooner or later the local bobbies are going to wake up to the fact that they've lost their ladies, and presuming the ladies told someone where they were going, sooner or later they're going to come round here asking questions. They might even get a warrant. We certainly don't want that car here then."

"I will see to it at once, Mr. Grieg."

"Good. Ozols and Pētersons, keep our guests covered and stay sharp. I don't trust them. Especially not the boss lady. I'll bet," he said, again addressing Cecilia directly, "given half a chance, you're trickier than a rattlesnake."

The observation seemed to call for no response, and Cecilia made none.

"Now, I'm going to give you ladies an order. And when you get it, you're to obey, but *move slowly*. Put your hands up over your heads where I can see them. That's right. Good. We're going for a ride in the elevator. Or, as we're in little old England, I guess maybe I should say the *lift*."

Cecilia barely stifled a sigh. The man clearly delighted in the sound of his own voice, but it was a weakness she could as yet see no way of exploiting. And Ozols's and Pētersons's weapons did not waver. In fact, she had the feeling that Ozols in particular would rather enjoy a chance to use his.

And so, deliberately, she willed herself to seem blank, uninteresting, not even worth the trouble of killing.

Grieg pressed a button, and the lift doors slid open.

"In you go, ladies. Slowly. Slowly. And straight to the back! No lurching toward the controls—you'll be dead before you've even started to work out how to use them. That's right. As for you, Cartwright, stay at your desk and try to look as if you're in control of something, even though we both know you aren't. Speak as little as possible. That way you're less likely to say something stupid. Another screw-up like this and I just might kill you myself."

Grieg, Ozols, and Pētersons followed them into the lift. Ozols and Pētersons continued to cover them while Grieg went to the control panel. Cecilia, her hands held high, managed to turn her head just enough to watch out of the corner of her eye as he selected a floor.

SIXTEEN

The Police Station, Edgestow. 11:20 a.m.

"Sergeant Wyatt, I'm sorry to bother you but I think something's wrong."

Joseph Stirrup stood leaning on his stick and looking somewhat out of breath.

The sergeant looked up from the files he was reading.

"Oh? What's the problem, Joseph?"

"Well, Sergeant, DS Jones has her phone synched to my computer. And mine's synched to hers."

Sergeant Wyatt suppressed a smile.

"The thing is," Joseph said, "hers has died. Gone off line, completely."

"Mayn't that just mean she's turned it off? Or the battery's dead?"

New love could get very anxious over very little.

"No, Sergeant. The battery isn't dead. I charged it myself last night and checked it for her this morning. So whether the phone's turned off or not, I should still be able to locate its *signal* within a few meters. It's automatic. That's why the link's so useful — Verity's always leaving her mobile somewhere and forgetting where she's put it. This way I can find it for her. But now there's nothing. No signal at all. It's as if the phone didn't exist — or as if someone had smashed it."

"Well, she's with DCI Cavaliere. Why not give her a call?"

"We can't, Sergeant—that's why I'm worried. Of course I don't have a computer link with DCI Cavaliere, but I did try calling her mobile and that appears to be dead too. And now it seems we can't raise the car radio, either. I could believe one system had accidentally gone on the blink, but all three at once? I don't think so."

Sergeant Wyatt got to his feet.

"I take your point, Joseph. All right, let's see. According to the log they were bound for the UN Institute, so let's give U.N.I.T.E.D. a call, shall we?"

SEVENTEEN

Edgestow, the U.N.I.T.E.D Central Tower. A few minutes later.

There was a single click, then seconds after closing, the lift doors slid back again, opening now onto a long well-lit room with large windows at each end. There was a desk, a chair, a door, and not much else. Behind the desk was another gray-uniformed security guard.

"Jansons," Grieg said, "these two ladies are dangerous. If you see them moving around without proper escort, shoot them. Dead. Got it?"

"Yes, Mr. Grieg." A similar accent.

They passed through the room and found themselves in a large windowless hall with another door at the far end. It could have passed for a hospital ward. There were beds down each side, prone figures on several of them. A white-coated man was checking charts. He looked up at their entrance and came towards them.

"Mr. Grieg," he said. "No developments, I'm afraid."

"No, Doctor Telfer—but do I have a development for you! Two new clients to be downloaded into the latest version of our program. Our first Caucasians! Our first females! How about that?"

The doctor looked at Cecilia and Verity, then at Balodis and Pētersons covering them with their weapons.

"For God's sake, Grieg," he said, "isn't this a hell of a risk? Who are these women? Surely someone's going to be looking for them?"

"It's a bit of a risk, yes. In fact it's worse than you think. They're actually cops. But the fact is, our perfect English gentleman colleague, asshole Louis Cartwright, has screwed up, and we got landed with them. So we may as well make use of them. I believe it's what our esteemed director would call turning a difficulty into an opportunity. Now, ladies," he turned again to Cecilia and Verity, "sit down over there."

He indicated some seats by the wall.

"Telfer, let's talk."

The two walked together to the other end of the hall. After a few minutes Grieg nodded and turned back to the two women. Before he could say anything, one of the security men entered from the door behind him and spoke softly in his ear.

He listened and nodded.

"All right," he said, "I'll take it myself. The rest of you, keep them covered."

Sergeant Wyatt found the switchboard at U.N.I.T.E.D. both responsive and efficient. They put him through at once to their main office. Within a few minutes he was speaking to a man called Herbert Grieg, who identified himself as assistant to the deputy director. He seemed to take the sergeant's concerns seriously and said he would have his people check.

For the next few minutes Wyatt listened to classical music. Mozart? Or was it Beethoven?

Then Mr. Grieg was back.

He was sorry, but they had no record of any visit to the institute by any police officers that morning. Their internal security was very efficient and there would certainly be a record of such a visit had it occurred. Was it possible the officers had been involved in an accident on their way? Would the police like the institute's own security people to check the surrounding area for them? They had the manpower available and could easily handle it.

The sergeant (who disapproved of security firms on principle, and of armed security firms in particular) declined the offer — the police would see to that.

Real police, not people pretending to be police.

Was there then any other way in which the institute could help locate the missing officers? They were anxious to assist law enforcement if that was possible.

No, the sergeant thought not. He thanked Grieg, hung up the phone, and considered.

The U.N.I.T.E.D. man had certainly been eager to help.

Maybe a bit too eager?

The next thing, in any case, was to send some officers and a patrol car to look for the two missing detectives. He glanced at the log. As he thought — Wilkins and Jarman were in the vicinity. They could start the search.

And then, given the situation, he needed to call Exeter.

EIGHTEEN

Edgestow, the U.N.I.T.E.D. Tower. A few minutes later.

"Well, ladies, some of your colleagues seem to be concerned about you. Touching, isn't it? Fellow calling himself Sergeant Wyatt telephoned. Anyway, I explained to him in my most convincing tones that you hadn't been seen here, which seemed to satisfy his curiosity. My guess is they're not the sharpest knives in the drawer, your Sergeant Wyatt and his friends. Anyway, I dare say you're both wondering what all this is about."

True enough.

But Cecilia contented herself with saying, "Is this the kind of thing Sir James Harlow encourages you to do, using people in your programs whether they're willing or not?"

"No, of course it isn't. The virtuous Sir James is a useful figurehead. But he's far too busy organizing international peace and goodwill to have time to run this place. The only ones apart from me and Telfer who actually know what's going on here are friend Cartwright—who is, as you saw, an idiot—and of course my nine fine Latvians, who do as they're told and don't ask questions."

It must be tricky, though, hiding all this from someone as astute as Sir James, even if he was only at the institute occasionally. Especially when your main colleague was an idiot?

"Now," Grieg said, "I don't suppose either of you ladies has any idea what a singularity is?"

It's what Jane Austen says *often makes the worst part of our suffering, as it always does of our conduct,* but I doubt that's the answer you're after.

Verity, however, appeared to be more on Grieg's wavelength.

"It's a theoretical point in space-time," she said, "where gravity distorts time, space, and matter so much that you can't predict events by the normal laws of physics. Technology has borrowed the term to mean a theoretical point in the emergence of super-intelligence where you can't predict events because human minds can't comprehend such an intelligence."

Grieg stared at her, then looked at Cecilia.

"Hey, boss detective lady! I guess your sidekick's had some education."

Cecilia resisted a temptation to point out that her "sidekick" had a double first in *litterae humaniores* from one of the world's great universities.

But Grieg had already turned back to Verity.

"So, sidekick lady, you say 'theoretical point' in both cases. Do you think the theories might have any basis in reality?"

"I haven't studied enough in either discipline to have an opinion that would be of any value."

Oh Verity, Verity, I do wish I had the ability to sound so prim and proper while at the same time gazing upon the world with the appearance of such wide-eyed innocence.

Grieg, however, had clearly received from this all the encouragement he needed and was now on a roll.

"Well, honey, let me put you right. Evidently, since you know about the technological singularity, you've heard something about the inevitability that we will in a few years develop computers that will equal and then surpass the human brain. Well, all that's more or less right—except that it's way *behind* the reality. We've *already* developed it. Everything that a human being is — all the thoughts, ideas, hopes, emotions, and dreams, everything that's contained in that admittedly rather remarkable computer that is the human brain — all that can now be downloaded into this even more remarkable computer we've built here at the institute."

He pointed to the console and control panels to his left.

"Behold — Advanced Digitally Automated Mind Prototype 1, known for short as A.D.A.M.1. Be in awe."

He paused — almost as if he were expecting applause.

After a moment, he continued.

"So — where next? There are various ways this may go. On the one hand, we *can* undoubtedly create a machine that is equal to and even superior to ourselves, a personality. We are almost there. Intelligent life, consciousness, and so on will no longer be matters for psychologists and religious fanatics to rave about but matters of scientific and mathematical formulae, graspable and repeatable.

"But there's also the matter of our own mortality. This is what interests me particularly, what primarily drives my work here. Indeed, it's what's driven my work for the last decade. Until now, death has been regarded as inevitable and universal. No longer! Some of my colleagues believe the human body itself can be indefinitely fixed and repaired with better parts, just as we do with a vintage car to keep it going. Personally I doubt that — the human body is just too weak, too full of obvious design flaws, for that to be practical. Another view — and this is my opinion — is that the thing to do is to discard the body altogether. We must download ourselves, all that we have in our brains, onto a computer in a robot body — infinitely stronger and infinitely more durable than a human body. The robot body need *never wear out*. And so we'll have achieved immortality!"

Verity stared at him.

Cecilia looked at Verity.

Grieg sailed on.

"While the theory of downloading information from one computer—in this case the human brain—to another is, of course, quite straightforward, what we need are details as to how it's experienced from within. So far our attempts to obtain those details have failed. The first half dozen we tried to download into ADAM1 simply died. We made adjustments and the second lot did regain consciousness, but the subjects were deranged and violent. We had to shoot them—all six of them. It was disappointing, to say the least."

At this revelation—delivered in tones that would have been appropriate had he been complaining about the quality of service in a restaurant or the lateness of an airline flight—Cecilia felt for the first time a prickle of real fear on the back of her neck. This man wasn't just a criminal egomaniac. He was a killer, and he had absolutely no conscience at all.

"We've made some more adjustments, and our third group"—he indicated the figures in the beds—"so far seems more promising. None of them has died. Doctor Telfer is maintaining them with nutrients and liquids. But none of them has regained consciousness, either. Of course, and as Dr. Telfer constantly reminds me, we have to be patient. We're on the edge of entirely new modes of being and can't expect to have everything work the first time. Cultural and sexual differences may also be affecting the experiment. That's where you come in. You will be our first Caucasians, our first westerners, and our first females. That introduces new factors and may be just what's needed to produce the results we need."

Cecilia nodded. Horrifying though Grieg's perception of the matter was, it was clearly also the thread to which he had referred, the thread by which her and Verity's lives now hung. She dare not disturb it.

"Here's what I hope will happen," Grieg said. "We've programmed the computer so that what you should experience when you're downloaded into it will, in effect, be a kind of game. The game will be based on something in your own psyche—a past experience, a belief, a family tradition. The computer, having access to all your data, will have analyzed it and come up with a suitable scenario. It will place you in this scenario. You must play through the situation and win, in order to complete the program and automatically be uploaded again back to your body. It doesn't matter what actually happened historically, of course. It will be like those computer games where you reenact great battles of the past—Civil War battles, for example. You can replay Gettysburg, and this time maybe you can make it so that the Confederates win."

"What happens if we refuse to play?" Verity said. "Or if we lose?"

"Well, that's a tough one, I'm afraid. You can't refuse to play, of course, because you'll be *in* the program, not outside it choosing whether to turn it on or off."

"And if we lose?"

"If you *lose*—say, you go and get yourself killed—then the computer will delete you. Which we'll know, because your body here will die. We've had to program it like that, you see, in order to give our clients some incentive to play—and play as well as they can. Otherwise they might just give up and return to their bodies. And we can't have that, can we?"

"Certainly not," Verity said. "That would be no fun at all."

Grieg frowned.

"The point is," he said, "it wouldn't tell us what we need to know."

NINETEEN

J oseph reappeared just as Sergeant Wyatt decided he needed to call Exeter.

"Sergeant, may I ask what the people at U.N.I.T.E.D. said?"

"They'd no news of them. I talked to the assistant to the deputy director. He checked with their security people and they said they'd no record of any visit by any police to the complex this morning."

Joseph shook his head.

"Well, Sergeant, either the assistant to the deputy director wasn't telling you the truth or his security people weren't telling *him* the truth."

"Why do you say that?"

"Because while you were on the phone, I went back to my computer and checked through the history for this morning. I've programmed Verity's phone to send its signal every hour, on the hour. Her phone sent out a signal at ten a.m., and according to that signal they were already inside the institute then. They *did* visit there this morning, whatever U.N.I.T.E.D.'s security or their assistant director or whoever he is says. And if they've got security posted at their entrance, they must know that."

"Now Joseph, steady on. We're getting into deep water here. You're sure DCI Cavaliere and DS Jones were inside the institute?"

"I'm absolutely sure. Satellite positioning is never more than a few meters out at most, and it's not as if we were talking about a single building. The institute is a complex of buildings well over a mile across. Its perimeter is perfectly clear on the image I have, and the last signal came from well inside it. I mean *well* inside. Half a mile or so. Almost at the center. Strictly speaking, I suppose I don't know whether Verity herself has been inside the institute complex this morning or not. But I'm perfectly certain that her phone has."

Sergeant Wyatt shook his head and sighed. Apparently that U.N.I.T.E.D. fellow really *had* been a bit too eager to help.

"Then it looks as though we've got a worse problem than I thought."

He looked at the wall clock. It was almost noon.

"Susan," he said to the secretary, who was typing notes, "will you please phone Chief Superintendent Davies in Exeter for me?"

Twenty

"Naturally," Grieg continued, still mainly addressing himself to Verity, "so long as we're in the experimental stage, before we risk a person of value to us we need to download people who can be disposed of—such as these illegals or now, I'm afraid, you. To do anything else would be foolish, so you needn't take it personally. And as someone who is at least partially educated, perhaps you can understand that what we're doing is justified by the enormous step forward we shall enable humanity to take. Every battle must have its casualties, but the cause at stake here is nothing less than the hope and future of the human race. Even you can't deny that's a cause worthy of some sacrifices."

There was a pause during which he stared at them both.

Was he waiting for applause?

Cecilia watched, fascinated despite herself as Verity, who seemed unfazed by the situation, stared back with the faintest of smiles.

"Mr. Grieg," she said, "I don't even approve of vivisecting animals."

With which observation she switched her gaze from Grieg to the figures on the beds, as if he was no longer of interest to her.

Grieg snorted and shook his head.

"Fortunately not everyone thinks as prissily as you, or we'd still be living in the Middle Ages."

Verity was still looking at the figures on the beds.

"Personally," she said, "I've always rather admired the Middle Ages. But aside from that, don't even you from your non-prissy and thoroughly modern point of view think there's something wrong with taking advantage of all these people who've just come over here trying to make a better life for themselves?"

Grieg looked at her and sighed — a good teacher trying to be patient with a witless student.

"Basically," he said, "that's a question without meaning. You said it yourself — faced with this new level of intelligence, all our previous predictions are out of the window. Can't you see that this has to include our notions of so-called right and wrong? Ethics, philosophy, moral values, all the stuff human beings have believed in or thought they knew until now? We need to move *beyond* those concepts!"

That's exactly what my first husband George used to say, Cecilia thought. But she said nothing.

Instead, she looked at the figures on the beds. The nearest was turned towards her and she could see his face, the features strong, somewhat aquiline, and even in repose a good deal more interesting than those of their endlessly loquacious captor.

"What I'm talking about," Grieg said, "is humankind *transcending* those ancient notions of morality! I'm talking about *the species surviving in a new form.* And that's what I'm working to bring about."

"But *why?*"

Verity surprised Cecilia by leaning toward Grieg in what seemed for a moment like renewed interest, as if she had suddenly seen a point of possible connection between them.

"If you really believe there's no such thing as right and wrong," she said, "if all those old values are out of the window, why do you want the species to survive at all? What's the point of it?"

Grieg shook his head.

"Honey, you still don't get it, do you? There's no evidence of *any* point or purpose to biological evolution. But let's cut to the chase. I don't *care* whether there's any point to it. Survival of the species means survival of *some* of the species, and I intend to be part of that."

The door opened at the far end of the ward.

"Ah — and here comes Dr. Telfer, who's going to inject you both with a drug: ketamine, a dissociative anesthetic. It has no lasting effects — an hour or so at most — but it will temporarily relax you. Vets use it a lot. We shall then lay you down and wire you up for your person to be downloaded. The process for that is quite simple and requires nothing other than electrical pads. It's not even invasive."

That depends on what you mean by invasive.

"The drill, ladies, is just the same as when you were searched. The doctor will inject each of you in turn, and if either of you makes any resistance, Ozols and Pētersons here will shoot the other. Remember what I told you. I can carry on this research without you, just I was doing before you arrived. Assuming you *don't* do something to make us kill one or both of you, we've decided to wire you up in parallel, which means you'll go in as a pair. We *think* this means that you'll both participate in the same scenario, taken from the life or family history or beliefs of one of you. And as we're going to put you in second, boss lady — make you the culminating factor, so to speak, we *think* that'll make it your stuff that's drawn on. But we'll see. Very well, Doctor Telfer. Carry on, and..."

Cecilia sighed.

Douglas Grieg *would* still be talking.

But the voice she was hearing was Rachel's as she clung to her two days ago.

"*Mamma, mamma, non andare!*"

Twenty-One

Heavitree Police Station. 12:10 pm.

Chief Superintendent Glyn Davies frowned.

"So—Cavaliere and Jones are out of communication and we don't know why. Stirrup's sure they arrived at U.N.I.T.E.D. but U.N.I.T.E.D. denies knowing anything about them. And you've got Wilkins and Jarman out in a patrol car looking for them. Have I got that right?"

"Yes, sir," Sergeant Wyatt said. "Of course there may turn out to be some perfectly reasonable explanation for the whole thing. But it did seem odd. So I thought you ought to be told."

"You were quite right, Sergeant. And as soon as you have something from Wilkins and Jarman, let me know, will you? I want to be informed of any development."

"Yes, sir."

Davies replaced the handset and considered.

Two of his most reliable officers were not where they were supposed to be and were out of communication for no apparent reason. And that, as Sergeant Wyatt said, was odd. Of course, as the sergeant also said, there might be some perfectly reasonable explanation for the whole thing, and Glyn Davies was all in favor of reasonable explanations. But until that explanation surfaced, odd was still odd. Davies made no claim to intellectual brilliance or remarkable detective instincts, but he did believe in attending to detail. And he could smell a rat as well as anyone. If over twenty years in the force had taught him anything, it was that if something was odd, you were wise to give it a close look.

After a moment's further reflection he telephoned Michael Aarons, whom he had met socially on a couple of occasions.

"Michael, have you talked to Cecilia in the last hour or so?"

"I can't say I have. Is there a problem?"

"Probably not, but we seem to have lost contact. Do you have a mobile number for her?"

"Yes."

"Would you mind calling it for us?"

"Of course not. Just give me a few seconds, will you?"

The superintendent had to wait barely a minute.

"I'm sorry, but this one doesn't seem to be working either."

Davies was careful to keep his voice calm.

"Oh well, not to worry — it's probably the weather or atmospherics or something. These mobile phones are still not as reliable as we'd like them to be. I'm sure we'll be in touch with her soon. Sorry to have bothered you! Thank you for trying."

"You're very welcome."

Twenty-Two

Saint Mary's Rectory, Exeter. A few minutes later.

Following the chief superintendent's telephone call, Michael returned the handset to its stand and then sat staring at it.

In hope rather than expectation he picked up the phone and again tried Cecilia's mobile number—just in case.

Still there was nothing.

He sighed and replaced it.

The chief superintendent's manner had been warm, reassuring, and calm. He'd clearly done everything in his power to indicate that there was no problem, just a glitch.

All of which told Michael there *was* a problem, and Cecilia was in the thick of it. And why? At least in part, surely, because the wise and far-seeing Michael Aarons, that nonpareil of wit and cool reason, had encouraged her to be.

Oh, Lord.

Certainly whatever danger threatened Cecilia, she would face it with casual courage. She was brave, adventurous, tough, and resourceful—qualities he adored in her, and the more so since he reckoned to be totally lacking in them himself. And of course policing in Devon and Cornwall was not nearly so hazardous as it could be in other places. More times than he could remember he'd thanked God she wasn't a police officer in a major city like London, or worse still some country like the United States where they had no proper gun laws and any lunatic could buy an assault weapon.

Still, even in Devon and Cornwall, policing had its dangers.

Perhaps it was the loss of his parents when he was young that had taught him never to take the presence of anyone precious to him for granted—and certainly not Cecilia. One might call this insecurity or one might call it wisdom, but whatever one called it, it meant that he was invariably conscious each time he said goodbye to someone he cared about that it might be for the last time. Like yesterday evening, when he said goodnight to Cecilia on the iPad. He counted himself an extraordinarily happy man, yet was well aware that his happiness, like everyone's, hung by cords that could break or be broken at any moment.

He shook his head.

This was the bargain he'd made when she married him.

He frowned.

So... what?

So, whatever his anxieties, his present duty was to the shut-ins who had been promised Holy Communion that afternoon, including Mrs. Warterton, who was always in pain and always cheerful and a continual inspiration to him without, of course, the slightest intention of being anything of the kind.

He'd best commend Cecilia to God and get on with it.

And wasn't that, after all, the point of all the tough Ignatian spirituality that his guides at Farm Street had been endeavoring to teach him over the years? Wasn't it precisely so that he wouldn't drown as he so easily could, useless, in a rising tide of anxiety and panic? And had they succeeded? This, presumably, was one of the times when it would show.

Or not.

He got to his feet, stood stock still by his desk, and deliberately willed himself to be open as a channel of the divine grace to his wife, his beloved.

Lord, as you know her to be and not as I think of her, do, or do not do, as may be best for her.

He remained so for several minutes.

Until it seemed that he could do no more.

He sighed, and then went downstairs to the hall, which had a glass-paneled front door and lofty skylights and at this time of day was full of sunbeams and shadows. He took his cloak from behind the closet door, put it on over his cassock (the afternoon was fine and sunny, but chilly — the long hot summer seemed definitely to have ended), bade farewell to various cats and dogs (Mama was out with Rachel, and Papa was teaching), picked up his sick-communion case, and went out to the car.

He would do his job.

That, at least, he could manage.

And he must just accept as an unfortunate fact of life — indeed, an unfortunate fact about *him* — that even prayer and doing his job could not rid him of that tight, twisted feeling in his gut.

TWENTY-THREE

Apparently Rome. Il Ministero della difesa.
Evening, 8ᵗʰ September 1943.

Cecilia found herself apparently in a large room with a high ceiling and French windows opening onto a balcony. To judge by the light outside, it was either early evening or early morning. She looked down at herself and saw that she was wearing a military uniform. She was seated at a handsome though somewhat old-fashioned desk. Verity, wearing the uniform of an Italian officer, World War II, was standing in front of her and slightly to the side. Behind Verity was a cream-colored wall with a handsome double door. To the right of the door, a calendar with the date in Italian, 8 Settembre 1943; above the calendar, a crucifix.

There was a knock at the door.

"Come in," she said.

A soldier entered with a document. Verity moved aside, and he approached the desk.

"A draft of the accord as you requested, General. It's ready for you to look over."

"Thank you," Cecilia said, playing for time. "Leave it with me. I'll call you when I need you."

"Yes, General."

The soldier left.

"Do you know what's going on?" Verity asked. "Where are we? It's Italy, isn't it? This has got to be something to do with you. Grieg seems to have got that bit right."

"Yes," Cecilia said. "I suppose that means I ought to be able to work out what I'm supposed to do."

She gazed at her fingers and flexed them.

"Well," she said, "at least Grieg's drug doesn't seem to be affecting our movements."

Verity shrugged. "I don't think it would affect them in virtual reality ma'am, any more than it would in a dream. And virtual reality must be what this is, however real it seems."

Cecilia nodded.

She was worried and not a little scared. Even leaving aside Grieg's homicidal tendencies, so far, on his own admission, he hadn't once succeeded in getting anyone back from this experiment.

It was not a record to fill one with confidence.

She glanced at the document and read a few sentences. She turned a page and read a little more. Then she put it down, looked up at the date on the calendar, and pursed her lips.

"Just give me a minute," she said.

She got up from the desk, went to the window, and looked out at the scene below. Finally she turned back and looked at Verity.

"I know exactly what's going on," she said. "It's a part of my family history. We're in Rome. It's the evening of September the eighth, 1943. It's the day before my great-grand-uncle Andrea was killed — in a situation of total chaos, even by Italian standards."

Verity waited.

"As our family tell it," Cecilia continued, "in 1943, after Mussolini was overthrown, Prime Minister Badoglio signed an armistice with the Allies. That was on the third of September.

On the eighth — which appears to be today" — she pointed to the wall calendar — "the Allies published it. But believe it or not, in the intervening five days, Badoglio hadn't bothered to tell the Italian military. Nobody knew the truth. As a result the Italian army was completely unprepared. In the early hours of the ninth of September — that'll be tomorrow morning — Badoglio and various other people who were supposed to be running the show panicked and ran off to be safe with the Allies. They left behind them General Giacomo Carboni, who was supposed to be responsible for defending Rome. And the computer seems to have decided that I'm General Carboni."

"That soldier obviously thinks you're a general," Verity said. "You look just the same as ever to me — apart from the uniform, which I must say rather suits you."

"Thank you. And you look very elegant. But then I'd expect that, even in virtual reality."

"So — what happened?"

"What happened is that General Carboni was worse than useless. First he tried to run away with the others. Then when that didn't work he sat down in his office and made an agreement with the Germans so that they could take over Rome. He said he had no choice because the city couldn't be defended. So although some of the units he should have been commanding fought magnificently, my great-grand-uncle's unit among them, and were actually victorious in the field, Carboni sold them out."

"The Italians won the battle and then their own general betrayed them?"

"That's pretty well it. This" — Cecilia pointed to the document on the desk — "is a draft of his agreement with the Germans. It's all obviously pretty well drawn up. A done deal. He's planning to give Kesselring — that was the German general — everything he wants. There's a note here from Kesselring — you see? Kesselring says he's got heavy tanks stationed only eight kilometers from the city, here" — she indicated a point on the map—"and he's threatening to use them in the city if Carboni doesn't surrender it to him."

"So what are you going to do?"

"Well, I'm not going to surrender. We've been told this is a computer game, and we have to win it. So I presume we're to refight the battle. And I, I can assure you, am *not* going to be the General Carboni I've just told you about. Let's see what the computer thinks would have happened if Carboni had played the man and decided he *would* defend Rome."

"Sounds exciting."

"It should be. Though in view of what Grieg said about what happens if we lose, we'd better remember that the bullets will be real, at least for you and me. So—much as I like to live dangerously, we'd probably best avoid them."

"I'm for that, ma'am."

"And you'd better not call me 'ma'am.'"

"No, ma'am—*sir*!"

Cecilia smiled.

"Adjutant!" she called out.

The adjutant reentered.

"Sir!"

"Take this piece of paper away. Our troops need leadership and encouragement, not defeatist nonsense."

"But sir, I thought you said Rome couldn't be defended."

"Did I say that? I suppose I must have done. Maybe I meant I'm not sure Rome can be defended *successfully*. That's what we'll find out. But Rome *can* be defended, and it's going to be. This is not a hopeless fight. Now get me a car that'll take me to la Magliana. It's time these Italian soldiers knew their commanding officer is on the job."

The adjutant, who had looked depressed and then puzzled, suddenly smiled.

"Thank God!" he said. "Long live Italy! I'll get you that car, sir."

"It's obvious he really does think you're this Carboni fellow," Verity said. "Who is la Magliana?"

"It's not a who, it's a what. It's a district of southwest Rome, by the Tiber—Municipio 15. At this period, frankly, it was a dreadful slum, and Mussolini hadn't done a thing for it—pretended it didn't exist, that it wasn't really part of Rome. He'd put all the money into building that awful EUR monstrosity."

"Oh."

"But still, la Magliana's where the action was—or rather where it's going to be tonight in September 1943. It's the front line."

"And you are the gallant commander who's going to get them to hold it. Right. I wonder who I'm supposed to be."

"You," Cecilia said, "are General Carboni's equally gallant *aiutante di campo*, who will if necessary die with him in the breach, defending the eternal city against the barbarian hordes."

"I will? Oh, well that's all right then. I thought for a minute I might be in some kind of danger."

Twenty-Four

Apparently la Magliana, Rome. Later the same night.

It was dark and cold with a hint of rain when they drove into the piazza. There were soldiers everywhere. Verity peered up at what looked like a large church: a painted sign said, "Basilica di San Paolo."

Cecilia was quickly out of the car. Verity joined her.

A young officer approached.

"General! It's good to see you here!"

"Thank you. Where is your commander?"

"In the command and control center, sir. I'll take you there at once, sir."

They found the commander studying a map in a small room at the base of the basilica. He looked up at them, obviously surprised.

"General! This is an honor—"

"What's the situation, commander?"

"I have to admit, sir, we've had a setback. German paratroops have occupied Caposaldo five on the Via Ostiense. That gives them control of the bridge and easy access to the city. And they've taken some of the Granatieri prisoner. Sir, they only managed it because they pulled a trick on us—"

"What's past can't be helped, commander. What are you proposing to do about it?"

"Take it back, sir."

"Good. What's the plan?"

"I'm bringing up the second cadet battalion of the Carabinieri. They should be pretty well in place by now. We've also got a battalion of *Polizia dell'Africa Italiana*, a unit of the *Lancieri di Montebello*, and parts of the first and second battalions of the Granatieri that didn't get captured. I think it's enough, sir. The Granatieri are mad as hell at the trick the Germans played on their comrades—they're just itching for a fight. So are the Carabinieri. I really think we can do this, sir, if you'll just let us try."

General Carboni's reputation for backing down to the Germans was clearly known, and it was obvious the commander was afraid his general was about to tell him to stand down.

But Cecilia said, "That's excellent, commander. I *know* we can do it. Let's get on with it."

The other's relief was palpable.

"Thank you, sir! We won't let you down."

"I know you won't. When do you plan to attack?"

"0600 hours, sir. I was just going to speak to the men and make sure everything's in place."

"Good. But before you do, I have just one other little project I'd like to discuss with you. God forbid I should weaken our attack force, but I'm wondering if we could spare a few men for something else."

"General?"

"Let's look at your map, commander, and I'll explain what I have in mind."

Verity could not hear what next passed between, but after a few minutes the commander nodded grimly, then smiled.

"Brilliant, sir! The last thing they'll expect. Definitely worth a try! We can spare the men for it. And if they do pull it off, it'll be a masterstroke."

"There'll need to be some who know how to drive those things."

Again the commander smiled.

"I've got lads who can drive anything that was ever given wheels. Don't worry about that, sir."

He summoned an orderly and gave instructions Verity didn't catch.

"Good," Cecilia said when he appeared to have completed the arrangements. "And now, we need to speak with the men. They need to know how much their general honors and trusts them — and that they're going to win. Let's go and tell them."

Twenty-Five

"Thank you, Susan. That's kind of you."

Without really tasting it, Joseph chewed on the slice of pizza the secretary had brought him and gazed blankly out of the trailer window. Someone had hung a birdfeeder full of peanuts on a pole in the grassy space in front of the trailer, and a flock of small birds were whirring and tweeting around it, enjoying the feast.

Verity would know what kind of birds they were.

She was a country girl at heart.

Verity… that funny little Welsh blonde who had a mind like a steel trap and was always quoting bits of Latin and who watched *Star Trek* and *Deep Space Nine* with him and who for the last year or so had brought her flask of coffee to share with him every morning when she was in the office and who was — it now crashed in on him as something he'd known for some time in his heart but had until this precise instant refused to admit — the lodestar of his life.

And he hadn't a clue where the hell she was.

Or, more to the point, whether she was okay.

He drew in his breath sharply and clenched his fists, aware

of mounting anger and frustration. Then sat up straighter in his chair, slowly flexed his fingers, and took hold of himself.

If Verity Jones was in trouble, Joseph Stirrup sitting in front of a computer working himself into a froth about it wasn't going to help her.

But Joseph Stirrup using his brains just might.

So then—what did they know?

On his own initiative he'd already done a bit of research about the people who were in charge of U.N.I.T.E.D.

The results were somewhat puzzling.

Sir James's background was, of course, impeccable, his service to the world and to the nation in the fields of international and domestic relations widely documented. His deputy Louis Cartwright, while hardly so impressive as Sir James, was also an understandable choice—the cadet of an old and distinguished Catholic family, friend of Sir James since Oxford. No doubt entirely suitable for his role at U.N.I.T.E.D.

It was Herbert Grieg who was the puzzle.

Certainly Grieg had proper qualifications for the U.N.I.T.E.D. job—in particular, for the part involving computers, the part that had interested Joseph from the beginning. Grieg's background, following education at a good private school in Saint Paul, Minnesota, had been solidly MIT. He'd received his Bachelor of Science degree in 1996, graduating *magna cum laude.*

Magna, but not *summa*, Joseph noted. Good, but not the best—was that significant?

Grieg had gone on to become Master of Science in 1998 and Doctor of Science in 2003, and after that until five years ago he'd been teaching and participating in MIT's research programs, working on the development and enhancement of magnetic core memory.

So far, it was all more or less what one would expect.

But then, abruptly, in the middle of the fall semester of 2008, Grieg had left MIT.

The puzzle lay in what happened next. Or rather what didn't happen. Between Grieg's leaving MIT in 2008 and his appointment to U.N.I.T.E.D. in 2012, Joseph could find no record of his having held any appointment of any kind, or of his being anywhere. None of the usual sources produced any information at all. It was as if the man had simply vanished for four years.

Vanished into thin air.

Which was unlikely.

Whether any of that had any bearing on the disappearance of Verity and Cecilia wasn't clear.

But it was certainly puzzling.

And if Joseph had learned anything at all from his friendship with Verity and Cecilia, it was surely that when one was trying to solve a mystery, anything that was puzzling was precisely the thing one ought to follow up.

He had contacts in the FBI, Interpol, and Europol.

Surely someone among them must know something?

Clearly, he had a lot of telephone calls to make.

Twenty-Six

Apparently La Magliana. 9th September 1943.

"What's this *Caposaldo*?" Verity asked Cecilia as they walked back through the lines. "The commander obviously thinks it's important."

"It is," Cecilia said. "It's a small fortification but it commands the entrance and exit to the city. The commander's quite right. They've got to recapture it."

"You seem very confident that they will."

"I *am* confident. All this part of the computer program really happened — except that the real General Carboni wasn't encouraging his troops, he was cowering somewhere in the background betraying them to the Nazis. I told you, this is part of my family history. The night my great-uncle was killed, the Italian troops defending Rome had the Germans whipped. Even the Germans admitted that. But then Carboni sold them out and made Rome a so-called 'open city' — which was a sham and everyone knew it. So now you just watch! Our men will retake Caposaldo Five tonight. They will, because they did. As I said, the big change is that I'm cheering them on, and I can't believe that's going to make them fight *less* well than they fought without encouragement."

When they arrived at their destination a small group of officers gathered around them.

"Do you have new orders for us, sir?" one of them said cautiously.

"Basically there's just one order, and you already have it," Cecilia said. "Take back that damned Caposaldo Five, then hold on to it!"

Her questioner looked relieved. Several of the other officers grinned and nodded.

"Yes, sir!"

"You can count on us, sir!"

They were ardent, eager young men—no doubt just the sort of ardent, eager young men, proud of their country and willing to defend it with their lives, as the real General Carboni had sold out to the Nazis. At the thought, Cecilia's mouth tightened and her eyes narrowed.

"Sir?" one of them said, "Are you all right?"

"Yes," she said, taking a grip on herself. "Yes! And I *know* I can count on you. You are the best of the best. Some of you may have heard rumors that we're about to surrender. Well I'm here to tell you that so long as I'm in command, we'll never surrender. We'll fight the Germans street by street if we have to, but we'll never give them Rome. This isn't the first time the eternal city has been attacked by barbarians, and it won't be the first time she's thrown them back. Go to your men and tell them that what they do tonight will not be forgotten. They fight as Romans. And they will win. *Victory is the slave of Rome.* God bless you all."

She turned to the dark face of the officer of the *Polizia dell'Africa Italiana*—whose features seemed vaguely familiar to her.

"I see, sir, that you're an African," she said, "and I trust you are proud to be one. But I hope that tonight you will also be proud to be Roman, for all who defend the eternal city are Roman."

He grinned and saluted.

"I shall be proud to be Roman, my general."

TWENTY-SEVEN

Heavitree Police Station.

PCs Wilkins and Jarman did their best. They assiduously checked both obvious and not so obvious routes from the Edgestow Police Station to the U.N.I.T.E.D. complex and questioned everyone they came across. They pursued the matter for the best part of two hours, and came up with nothing.

Well, not quite nothing.

A couple of farm workers in a field remembered seeing two young women, a brunette and a blonde in a blue Ford Fiesta going in the direction of the U.N. complex. They remembered them because they'd reckoned them both to be quite fancyable.

"With your lot, are they?" one of the workers said, "Well, I tell you what, constable—any time you want to bring me in for questioning, you just send that little blonde to get me and I'll come quiet!"

His companion guffawed.

The farm workers weren't entirely sure of the time they'd seen the women, but they reckoned they'd put it a bit before nine.

When Sergeant Wyatt phoned Wilkins's and Jarman's report through to Chief Superintendent Davies with nothing more than this unhelpful fragment, Davies decided it was time to raise the stakes. He contacted the National Police Air Service. NPAS had an aircraft available and responded at once. Within minutes one of their blue and yellow Eurocopter EC145s was making repeated sweeps of the entire area. They worked at it for the best part of an hour. The sunny weather promised earlier by the meteorological office had now arrived, and visibility was excellent. But again, no joy. The two-person crew could see nothing relating to the missing officers or the blue Ford Fiesta.

This then was the situation that faced the chief superintendent at mid-afternoon, when one of the secretaries took pity on him and brought him a cup of tea and a chocolate digestive biscuit.

He thanked the secretary, ate the biscuit, drank the tea, and considered.

He had two missing officers.

According to Joseph Stirrup, the U.N.I.T.E.D. complex remained the last place where they had been and from which they had made contact.

"What we need," he said aloud, "is a search warrant."

But did he have enough evidence to get one?

True, he smelled a rat.

But the fact was, his case for involving U.N.I.T.E.D. had only two strands: the evidence connecting them with the illegal immigrants provided by the GPS navigator, which was circumstantial at best, and Joseph Stirrup's tracking report—that is, the assertion of one civilian computer specialist who *could* have made a mistake and who was contradicted by the officials of U.N.I.T.E.D. itself. For his part, he'd never known Joseph to make a mistake about something like this—well, about anything—and he trusted his expertise. The judge, however, would not have that advantage.

Davies sighed and shook his head.

He needed something more. And he hadn't the slightest idea where he was going to get it.

His outside line was flashing. He picked up the handset.

It was a woman from the Road Crash Investigation Team, calling to give him the latest developments in the matter of the white van. There were several, some serendipitous, some the result of careful police work.

A woman and her dog out for a walk late yesterday evening had found a man's body in a ditch by a lane near the A30. She called the police, and the body turned out to be that of William Frasier, the missing driver of the van. It had been easy enough to establish his identity, even without the benefit of DNA. When police examined the body they found on him photo IDs—his passport and a driving license in his wallet. His brother had come down from London that morning and formally identified him. Some of the mud on William's shoes matched the mud on the grassy bank beside the motorway, and the shoes themselves matched the footprints they'd found there, even down to a small irregularity in the right sole.

Meanwhile forensics had established that William Frasier died of a massive cerebral edema, presumably caused by a blow received in the crash.

"Forensics' surmise," the woman from ARCIT said, "is that it was an example of what's called Second Impact Syndrome. They found evidence on the body of an earlier blow to the back of the head—a month or so ago—that could have concussed him. And his brother confirmed that this was precisely what had happened. He'd got himself into some kind of gang scrap, and the doctor said he had a concussion. There were no serious effects at the time, but then a second blow in the car wreck so soon after it was fatal."

"Yet he managed to climb out of a wrecked van and walk all that way? A bit surprising that, isn't it?" Davies said.

By which, he reflected, I mean that I haven't come across it before.

"Not especially. People playing contact sports have been known to continue playing after a second concussion and even walk off the pitch unassisted. But then once the symptoms start, they progress pretty rapidly and almost always end in death."

"So Frasier could have panicked—presumably because he knew what was in the van—and done a runner? And then collapsed?"

"Exactly. If he'd stayed where he was the medics might have been able to help him. Probably not, but they might—not to mention helping his unfortunate passengers. We'll never know. At least they could have made him more comfortable. As it was, he must have been feeling terrible—ghastly headache, nausea, dizziness, the lot. Till it got him."

"A miserable end," Davies said.

"Terrible. There's just one more thing, though, that we thought you'd want to know, in view of the evidence of the GPS navigator."

"Yes?"

"At 14.21 hours—that would be about five minutes after the crash—Frasier made a call on his mobile phone. It was to the United Nations Institute for Technological Experimentation and Development."

"Was it indeed?"

Davies smiled.

"*Yes!*" he said softly to himself with a gesture of triumph toward the ceiling.

"Sorry—what did you say?"

"Oh, nothing. But thank you *very* much. Could you fax me all this—especially about the phone call? ASAP? I think it's going to be very helpful."

"Of course. We'll send it straightaway."

The call finished, Chief Superintendent Davies sat for a moment without moving.

Then he got up from his desk and walked over to the fax machine, which after a few minutes began to hum.

He removed the documents one by one as they appeared and glanced through them, pausing a couple of times to read a paragraph more closely, making sure that he hadn't missed a detail.

Finally he shuffled the papers together and nodded.

This, surely, was the *something more* that he needed.

He returned to his desk and picked up the phone.

Twenty-Eight

Apparently La Magliana. 9ᵗʰ September, 1943.

"You're good at this," Verity said as they walked back toward the command and control center. "Perhaps you ought to have been a soldier."

Cecilia shook her head.

"Think what this is about—I mean, what it *was* about when it really happened. Even leaving aside the fact that the Italians are about to be betrayed—even leaving that aside, all these beautiful young men so full of life, the Italians *and* the Germans, they're all about to kill each other or be killed, when they could be at home making love or playing with their children or making music or doing a million other useful happy things. I think to command soldiers in war must be heartbreaking. I'm not sure I could stand it. I'm perfectly happy being a police officer, thank you. I don't want to fight wars. I want to keep the peace so that ordinary people can live in peace."

They walked on for a while in silence. Cecilia found herself thinking of times when she was little and she and her father read Shakespeare together. She remembered Bates, the ordinary soldier who speaks before the battle of Agincourt. Papà always liked to read that bit himself. She could hear him now:

"I am afeard there are few die well that die in a battle, for how can they charitably dispose of anything, when blood is their argument? Now, if these men do not die well, it will be a black matter for the king that led them to it."

She sighed.

Of course, Shakespeare then gave the king a long speech about how you couldn't blame the sender if his agent was bent. She usually got to read that part. It was clever. But it never seemed to her that it came within a mile of actually addressing Bates's point. Which she'd always suspected was Shakespeare's quiet way of saying he really thought Bates was right.

"Well," Verity said, "at least you wouldn't sell your troops down the river like this fellow Carboni did."

"No, I wouldn't do that."

As Cecilia was speaking, Verity experienced a kind of shimmer through all that surrounded her: the street, the sky, everything seemed for an instant to flutter, and then was as before — yet not quite as before, for it all now seemed sharper, rougher, more vivid. There was garbage in the road that she hadn't noticed earlier, and there were strong smells — pizza with garlic, and sewage.

"Hello, who's this?" Cecilia said.

A young man had stepped out of the shadows. He wore the uniform of a Carabinieri cadet and looked tense, tired, anxious.

Something about him at once reminded Verity of Cecilia's father — a younger version. And he looked at them in a way that was quite different from the way everyone else had looked at them so far.

"Buona sera, signore," he said.

Well, that was pretty different. Evidently he, at least, didn't think they were General Carboni and his aide.

***

Cecilia, too, had noticed the shimmer and the change in the atmosphere, and the young man reminded her, too, of her father.

"*Signore*," the young man said, "this is not a good place for women. You should both get out of here."

He was staring at her intently.

"*Signora*, forgive me—but do I know you? You look just like the old photographs of my great-aunt Cecilia when she was young. But you can't be her."

"No, I'm not your great aunt," Cecilia said, and hesitated. Finally she said, "Are you all right?"

He sighed and shook his head.

"To be truthful, *signora*, no, I'm not all right. This is a mess."

From somewhere beyond the church there was a sudden burst of gunfire that died away after a few seconds. He looked in the direction from which it came, listening. Then he looked back at Cecilia. When he spoke again, his words came in a rush.

"It's not that I mind fighting. I'm quite willing to fight for Italy, and I'm willing to die for Italy if I have to. But they say we're fighting for nothing. The general's going to sell us out. They say we'll die and be forgotten and it's all a waste of time and won't do any good. So what's the point of dying for that?"

Cecilia sighed.

"Well, I'm afraid some of what they're saying is true. Your general is a coward and a traitor and he *is* going to sell you out. But the other parts aren't true. The way the Carabinieri fight to defend Rome tonight will not be forgotten, Andrea, either by Italy or by the Carabinieri or by your family. By the way, you *are* Andrea Cavaliere, aren't you?"

He'd looked taken aback when she called him by name, but now he nodded.

"Yes, I am."

"And as you see, I know your name even though I've never met you before. Well, Andrea, believe me—you will be remembered as a hero. You'll die tonight fighting side by side with your comrades in a noble cause, defending the eternal city. And then in 1945 in a free Italy in a free Europe you'll be awarded, in memoriam, the *Croce di Guerra al Valor Militare*, and your family will treasure that medal and honor your memory."

"So the Germans won't win the war?"

"No, they won't. Even in 1943 they're starting to lose, you know."

"Yes, I rather think they are. So who are you? You do look very like my great-aunt in the photographs. That's a compliment, you know. She was reckoned to be a beauty."

Cecilia laughed.

"I'm not sure I'm supposed to tell you this, but nobody's said I mustn't, so—my name is Cecilia Anna Maria Cavaliere, and I am your great-grand-niece. I was born—or I will be born—in 1979, and I live in England. I've come to love the English—and the Welsh." She smiled at Verity. "Indeed, I'm married to an Englishman. But I never forget that I am Italian."

He broke into a broad grin and shook his head.

"I think that's the most unbelievable story I've ever heard, and yet—though I can't say why—I believe you. And you've certainly cheered me up."

She smiled.

"So we're related?" he said.

She nodded.

"And I'm to die tonight—but a hero?"

She sighed, and nodded.

"Then give me a hug and a kiss, beautiful relative, so that I may remember it as I fight, and die bravely, and thoroughly deserve my *Croce di Guerra*."

Cecilia hugged him and kissed him. And then he was gone, as suddenly and quietly as he had appeared.

She and Verity walked on.

Again that sudden shimmer, and again all was as before. The smells of cooking and sewage had disappeared.

"Did you feel that?" Verity said.

"I did."

"Back there, just now, it all felt different—somehow more *real*. And that conversation you just had, that was entirely different from everything else that's happened here."

Cecilia looked at her.

"That gorgeous boy did *not* think you were a man," Verity said. "Or that I was. He called us '*signore*.' Even I understand enough Italian for that."

"Yes," Cecilia said with a smile, "that's true. He didn't think we were men."

"And that," Verity said, "is the other thing. You really spoke with him in Italian. All the time we've been here I've not thought about what language we were using—except maybe once or twice when you deliberately used an Italian phrase, like when you called me your gallant *aiutante di campo*. Otherwise it's as if the computer takes care of the language problem. But what happened just now with that boy was different. It was like it would have been in real life. I *knew* you were talking with him in Italian, and I understood some of it, but not enough to follow the whole conversation. He's your great-grand uncle, isn't he? The one who died in the defense of Rome?"

"He is," Cecilia said. "But as for the other things, I've no idea how to explain any of that. I simply told him the truth about the battle, and that he wouldn't be forgotten, and that seemed to cheer him up."

"I expect the kiss helped," Verity said.

TWENTY-NINE

Rachel was sitting on the carpet in Michael's study between Figaro and her teddy bear.

Michael had returned from his sick communion visits and was seated at his desk, signing letters.

Joseph Stirrup had phoned him shortly after he got home, and it had been some comfort to know that he wasn't the only one anxious about Cecilia and Verity. Joseph, for whose abilities he had enormous admiration, was clearly on the case, as were the rest of his colleagues.

The ormolu clock on the chimneypiece struck four.

Through the open door he could hear Cecilia's mama downstairs in the kitchen, filling the kettle, then setting out teacups.

"Daddy!"

"Yes, sweetheart?"

"Is mummy coming home soon?"

"Of course she is."

A pause.

"Daddy!"

"Yes, sweetheart?"

"*When* is mummy coming home?"

He hesitated.

"I'm not quite sure. Maybe next weekend? She said she'd be home every other weekend. Well, next weekend would be the first one, wouldn't it?"

He tried to sound casual, relaxed.

But Rachel had noticed his hesitation, or picked up on his anxiety, or —

"Daddy, is Mummy all right?"

"Of course she is, sweetheart. She's fine. Absolutely! But Mummy has to do her job. She has to keep us all safe. That's what she's busy doing."

"Oh."

He turned back to his letters but watched her out of the corner of his eye.

Her lip was quivering. She picked up her teddy bear and hugged it fiercely.

Figaro put his head down on to the carpet and looked depressed.

Michael signed the last letter and sat back.

If she'd been older of course he'd have explained to her what was worrying him, or at least some of it. But that would mean admitting he didn't know where Mummy was. And at her age a lost Mummy would surely be terrifying.

As it was, he'd just lied to her. Which he hated. And in any case it hadn't worked. Clearly she wasn't buying it. She knew he was worried.

So, come to that, did Figaro.

They were both too damned intuitive for their own peace of mind. Or his.

On impulse, he got to his feet, crossed the room, and sat down beside them on the carpet.

For a moment he and his daughter sat looking at each other.

"Hug?" he said.

Rachel climbed onto him, put her arms around his neck, buried her face in his shoulder, gave a big sigh, and was still.

He gave a big sigh of his own.

So they sat there.

Figaro thumped his tail.

The truth was, he felt better. It wasn't that he was no longer worried or that the tight, twisted feeling in his gut had gone away. No, it definitely wasn't that. But in a manner that he couldn't explain it did help to have Rachel sitting on him while Figaro thumped encouragingly at his side.

Having a hand to spare, he naturally reached it out and scratched Figaro's head.

When he stood up from his desk and crossed the room, he'd thought to comfort Rachel and Figaro.

Evidently he'd got it the wrong way round.

THIRTY

Apparently La Magliana, 9th September 1943.

Cecilia had known the story of the battle for Caposaldo 5 since she was a child. Yet still she was nervous as she took her place in the command and control center at La Magliana. She must win the game if she and Verity were to get out of Grieg's program alive, and since the program had cast her as the Italian general in command, she supposed that meant she must win this battle.

As the Italians had won it in 1943.

But if this were truly a game she had to win, that must mean that regardless of what had once happened in the real world, in the here and now it was possible for her to lose.

So suppose she made some dreadful mistake in her conduct of the battle?

It must surely be to her advantage that she knew in advance what the enemy was going to do.

Or did she?

What if the computer program changed something in the Nazi tactics?

Could it do that?

Would it do that?

She could see only one way to find out.

"The German paratroopers," she said, turning to the Carabiniere commander, "if I were them, I'd try to infiltrate our positions as our men are getting ready to attack. Warn the cadet Carabinieri to be ready for them. My guess is they'll come at us about thirty minutes before we plan to move—0530."

"Understood, General."

The commander passed on her instructions.

"Understood," came back over the radio.

There followed what seemed a long wait, though it could not have been more than fifteen minutes; then, at 0531, a burst of gunfire from the direction of the front line.

It appeared the computer program was playing fair.

Infuriatingly, at that precise moment they lost radio contact.

Sporadic bursts of gunfire.

White noise from the speaker.

The gunfire died away.

Silence.

She exchanged a look with Verity.

Abruptly, the speaker crackled into life.

"The krauts tried it, sir!" The voice was excited and slightly breathless. "Just like the general said they would! Tried to break into our flank! No problem, though. Once they realized we were onto them they gave up pretty quickly. Not many casualties on our side and we've taken most of them prisoner. The captain says thanks for the warning. He says it really helps when you've some idea what the other lot's going to do!"

Cecilia exchanged another look with her gallant *aiutante di campo*, who said, "Good start, General!"

Cecilia—*General* Cecilia as she was even beginning to think of herself—smiled grimly.

It was a good start.

But they weren't out of the woods yet.

At 0600 hours she nodded to the Carabinieri commander.

As planned, he gave the order to attack, and the Carabinieri cadets advanced, their right flank protected by the Tiber and their left by units of the Montebello Lancers and the *Polizia dell'Africa Italiana* — exactly as they had in the real battle.

The computer didn't play her false.

The conflict was fierce, but the cadets fought magnificently — again, just as they had in the real battle. By a little after 10.30 they'd overrun the German positions. They then pressed on beyond the Caposaldo and were able to liberate a number of Italian military who'd been taken prisoner as well as take many German prisoners and force the remaining Germans to retreat. There was more intense fighting, until eventually they were relieved by a fresh contingent of two hundred Carabinieri of the Pastrengo squadron. These successfully held the ground won by their young comrades, repelled two further attacks by the paratroopers, and finally compelled the Germans to a definitive withdrawal.

The Italians had won.

Such was the basic narrative, just as Cecilia had always heard it. What the narrative did not convey was the mind-pounding pressure of the experience. It didn't convey the tension of trying to stay focused for several hours through the rattle of gunfire and the thud and stink of high explosives. It didn't convey the anxiety of losing radio contact at what invariably seemed like crucial moments or the misery of seeing tired and sometimes desperately wounded men en route to and from the battle. It didn't convey the strain of needing at one moment to encourage and exhort, at another to stay calm, at another to give praise, while always appearing to be in control, on top of everything. Above all it did not begin to convey her emotions when in the bright light of morning the elite Pastrengo squadron arrived to reinforce her weary troops: two hundred men, well trained and well equipped, fresh and eager, at just the moment she needed them. After the shortest of briefings she ordered them into battle to the much-needed relief of their young comrades who had fought so well.

All these pressures, burdens, and occasional exhilarations of command she experienced over the best part of six hours. Only when the Italian victory was beyond doubt did she feel able to sit back and relax, just a little.

Even then she was not finished.

Now there were officers coming into the command center to make their reports. There were men to congratulate — young men who'd gone into the conflict as boys and returned as veterans. There were hands to shake. Heroes to embrace. Salutes to return.

Some of the heroes were terribly wounded.

There were stretchers. Some of them were covered.

Here was the Carabiniere commander who'd been at her side for most of the night and much of the morning. He looked exhausted but satisfied.

"I thank you, my general," he said. "Your dispositions have been superb."

"Thank you, Commander. But it was *your* dispositions that set us up. Have you news yet of our other little project?"

"Not yet, General."

"Let me know when you do."

"Understood, General."

And here was the dark, smiling face of the officer of the *Polizia dell'Africa Italiana* she'd spoken to before the attack.

"Well done," she said. "They tell me your men fought superbly."

His smile broadened.

"We are African and Roman, my general!" he said. "We have defended the eternal city."

"You have indeed. Now all of you — get some rest and some food."

He left, and again Cecilia had the odd feeling that she'd seen him somewhere before.

At this point another of her men — *another of her men? Good God, it was Verity!* — brought her a panino filled with *porchetto*, and wine in a tin cup.

"Bloody good show, sir," she said quietly — Verity was clearly "in role," as the actors say. "Our chaps beat the crap out of them. But you need to eat."

Cecilia took a sip of wine and a bite from the panino. The wine was cheap and the panino felt as if it had been made the day before, and since this was only a simulation presumably she wasn't actually eating or drinking either of them. Nonetheless she felt hungry, and through some miracle of electronic programming (for which, she supposed, she must thank Herbert Grieg) at this moment both tasted good enough.

She was exhausted.

And all she had experienced was the simulation of a battle.

God alone knew what the reality must be like.

She took another bite of panino and chewed slowly.

No, that wasn't true.

Many perfectly ordinary people knew what the reality was like. They'd fought at Marathon or Agincourt or Dunkirk or any of the other bloody horrors that mark the madness of human history.

Including, of course, Caposaldo 5 in September 1943.

She recalled the ninety-year-old Normandy veteran she'd recently seen on television who'd exchanged fire with a German soldier as they advanced. As he came up to the body he saw that the man he'd killed could not have been older than nineteen. Even now — almost seventy years on — he broke down and wept at the memory of that boy's face.

He knew the reality.

And so did the boy he killed.

"Sir," Verity said, "I've taken the liberty of finding out what happened to Cadet Andrea Cavaliere. I thought you'd want to know."

"Thank you," Cecilia said.

Verity produced a piece of paper and read from it:

"During military actions involved in the recapture of Caposaldo Five on the ninth of September 1943, Carabinieri

Cadet Andrea Cavaliere twice rescued wounded comrades under fire and on each occasion was commended by the officer commanding him in the field. The same officer reports that Cadet Cavaliere subsequently singlehandedly neutralized a German machine-gun post that had been holding up the Carabinieri advance. A few minutes after this exploit a stray shot mortally wounded Cadet Cavaliere and he died in the arms of a comrade, who described him as smiling in his last moments and apparently calling upon St. Cecilia for her prayers."

Verity looked up.

Cecilia gazed at her for a moment, then slowly raised the cup of wine.

"To Andrea Cavaliere," she said, and drank.

Verity nodded.

I am afeard there are few die well that die in a battle.

Andrea Cavaliere, it seemed, had beaten the odds.

Thirty-One

Exeter Crown Court, that evening.

A special sitting of the magistrate's court was convened for 8.30 p.m. — the earliest time the judge could be available. This was later than Chief Superintendent Davies would have liked, but a good deal better than nothing. The judge was to be Sir John Hull, a stickler for the law and for procedure, but always fair. Davies was not unhopeful.

Present were the judge himself with a clerk to the court, the chief superintendent, and a lawyer from the Crown Prosecution Service. Also present was Joseph Stirrup, who'd been driven over from Edgestow, Davies reasoning that Stirrup could present his technical evidence far better than anyone else could.

The judge listened attentively, from time to time making notes, as the chief superintendent outlined his reasons for suspecting that the U.N.I.T.E.D. complex was holding two of his officers, that an investigation of the complex was likely to produce evidence of this, and that U.N.I.T.E.D. and those representing it were unlikely to cooperate with the police in pursuing such an investigation.

The judge listened equally attentively to Joseph Stirrup's account of his discoveries that morning, put a couple of questions to him when he'd finished, and seemed satisfied with the answers. It occurred to Davies, not for the first time, what an impressive young man Stirrup was. He was glad he'd decided to have him on hand.

The clerk to the court then caught the judge's attention and told him something Davies could not hear. The judge nodded.

"Very well. I will raise that point."

He turned to the chief superintendent.

"Chief Superintendent Davies, a question has been put to me as to the exact status of the United Nations Institute in respect of English law. To be precise, as an organ of the United Nations, does it have some degree of diplomatic immunity that would enable it to refuse a search warrant issued by this court—as in the case of a foreign embassy? I understand that a claim to such immunity has from time to time been made by some of the institute's employees."

"Sir," the chief superintendent replied, "with your permission, Mr. Stemp, from the Crown Prosecution Service, will address that question."

The judge nodded.

"Please proceed, Mr. Stemp."

Mr. Stemp rose to his feet.

"Sir," he said, "the Crown Prosecution Service submits that diplomatic immunity, as agreed in international law at the Vienna Convention on Diplomatic Relations in 1961, is, and is only, a policy agreed upon and operative between governments. Its purpose is to allow for the maintenance of relations between governments."

The judge nodded.

"In the case of the United Nations Institute for Technological Experimentation and Development, it is true that the Home Secretary has granted a privilege normally associated with foreign embassies, in that he has allowed it to have its own armed security. That, however, is the *only* privilege the Home Secretary has granted. The institute does not represent a foreign government, its employees are not accredited diplomats, and its premises are not accredited as an embassy. Therefore, sir, the Crown Prosecution Service submits that in the institute's case the provisions of diplomatic immunity are irrelevant. U.N.I.T.E.D. and its employees have no basis in English or international law for claiming such immunity and are thereby subject to any search warrant issued by an English magistrate pursuant to the police carrying out their duties."

"Thank you, Mr. Stemp. That is very helpful."

The judge made another note, turned to his clerk, and conferred briefly.

He turned back to the court.

"Chief Superintendent Davies," he said, "I hope that you find your missing officers alive and well. In the meantime, you have your search warrant."

THIRTY-TWO

Apparently Rome. Il Ministero della Difesa. 9th September 1943.

"So what now?" Verity said.

There were back in the general's office overlooking the piazza.

"I mean," she added, "I know this is all a game and we're in a computer program, but it's so extraordinarily real I'm finding it easier and easier to think that you really are the general and that we really are in the middle of World War II."

"So am I," Cecilia said. "On the other hand, as for 'what now?' — I'm getting less and less sure every minute. We know, or at least we've been told, that I have to win the game. And since I'm General Carboni, and his responsibility was to defend Rome — successfully, presumably — I've been assuming that's how I win. So far it's been relatively straightforward because I knew more or less what our soldiers would do. The problem of course is that to do that I've also departed from history by urging the troops on instead of selling them out. And that means we're now in unknown territory. I don't know what the computer thinks would have happened if Carboni had done what he was paid to do, and I'm not even sure I know what it'll look like if I win the game. Maybe —"

There was a knock at the door.

"Come in! Adjutant?"

"Sir, the German commander is at our front line and demands you see him. Our men are holding him there but they're not sure what to do."

"Tell them they can join the club," Verity muttered.

"Generalfeldmarschal Kesselring is at our front line?" Cecilia said.

"Yes, sir."

Cecilia looked at Verity.

"Kesselring. Smiling Albert, they called him. He was an efficient soldier but a bloodthirsty one—responsible for several civilian massacres. Italian civilians."

She turned back to the adjutant.

"So he demands I see him, does he? All right, tell the men to let him through. And then see that as many men as possible are standing by to come in here if I need them. I'll see the field marshal, but I don't think I'll be telling him what he wants to hear. So perhaps he'll forget his manners."

Ten minutes or so later there was a sound of shouting from below, then stomping on the stairs. The door to the office burst open and a man in the uniform of a German field marshal stormed into the room.

"Carboni, what the hell is the meaning of this? We have agreed that Rome cannot be defended. I have your draft proposal. So why are your men not standing down? How dare you resist the Wehrmacht! I demand that you order your men to leave their positions immediately so that my troops can enter the city."

"Would you like to sit down, Albert?"

"I would not. I would like you to do as we agreed."

"As we agreed… now, that is interesting. How often you and your Führer have said that you don't trust the Italians! So how foolish to trust the word of an Italian officer! Tell me, Albert,

overall—not here in Rome at this moment, I admit, but overall—you Germans have us outgunned and outnumbered. Isn't
that true?"

"Of course it is true. The Wehrmacht is the greatest fighting
force in the world."

"Perhaps. I have nothing but admiration for the courage and
skill of your soldiers. But given we are outgunned and outnumbered, what weapon *do* we have?"

"You could behave with honor like a soldier."

"We have guile, Albert. We have guile. The weapon of those
who are otherwise at a disadvantage. And there is nothing dis-
honorable in using it. Ah! Here comes something interesting."

Both went to the French windows at the *very* loud roar of an
engine.

Onto the piazza below rumbled the formidable shape of a
German heavy tank: the feared Tiger I. Cecilia looked at it carefully. Kesselring gave it a quick glance.

"My tigers!" he said. "Good. Now you will stop this nonsense
or I will have them blow this piazza and every man, woman,
and child near it to pieces. So much for your eternal city."

"And so much for your soldier's honor," Cecilia said softly.

But there was only one tank, and she had noted that its
German cross was overpainted with a rough but unmistakable
Italian tricolor. She nodded to the adjutant, who was hovering
near the door, and at once the room began to fill with Italian
soldiers who came in quietly and stood waiting.

"I'm afraid you're wrong, Albert," Cecilia said. "There's just
one tiger, and it's mine."

She threw open the French windows and stepped out onto
the balcony. The tank's hatch squeaked and vibrated below.
Then it opened, and out of it emerged the head and shoulders
of an Italian *granatiere*, grinning broadly.

"Good morning," she shouted down.

"Good morning, General."

"I see your little expedition was successful."

"A walk in the park, sir. There were only a dozen of them on guard, they weren't expecting us, and they didn't want to put up a fight when they did realize who we were. So we took them prisoner and no casualties on either side. There are five more of these things. The commander's placed them at the San Paolo gate, covering the approach to the city—frankly, if you ask me they're better artillery than they are tanks. But he thought you ought to see one of them, just so as you'd know your plan worked."

People who had fled the piazza at the appearance of the tank were beginning to reappear. A couple of old men came out carrying a large tricolor flag, which they proceeded to drape over its front.

At which point Kesselring went for his pistol, but the young soldier beside him was quick enough to pinion his arms before he could reach it. A second removed the weapon from its holster.

"Well done!" Cecilia shouted down to the tank. "Congratulate your comrades for me!"

"Thank you, General. I will."

She turned back into the room.

The field marshal, helpless between the two stalwart lads who had pinioned and disarmed him, fumed and spluttered.

"I am a German officer. I demand to be released and treated in accordance with my rank and the honors of war."

Cecilia looked him up and down.

"I marvel, sir, that you dare to speak to me of honor when you've attacked my city without defiance offered or war declared. Even your Führer was prepared to withdraw to the north. But you, Kesselring? No, you had to conquer Rome. And now that you've failed—and in doing so sacrificed the lives of many of your own good paratroopers as well as my carabinieri—now that you've failed, you have the gall to come in here complaining. No, Kesselring, I will not accord you the honors of war. You did not *ask* to see me, you *demanded*. You came here under no flag of truce, you asked for no safe conduct, and I certainly offered you none. You swaggered in as if you were the victor, which you are not."

"One victory hardly makes *you* the victor, General."

"No, it doesn't. But it's a start. And in the meantime *you* are merely a man who's organized the massacre of Italian civilians. And in the name of the Italian people I am arresting you for that crime."

She turned to the soldiers holding the field marshal.

"Take this man away and lock him up. I've no further time to waste on him today. Oh, and tell his driver he's free either to return with their car to the German lines—I grant him safe conduct if he wishes to do that—or if he chooses he may surrender to you, in which case he'll remain here as a prisoner of war and be treated in accordance with the Geneva conventions. It's his call."

"Sir!"

The soldiers tramped out, taking Kesselring with them.

Cecilia and Verity were alone, Cecilia with a grin on her face.

"Now *that*, I must admit, felt like winning!" she said.

Verity smiled.

"As you said, ma'am, you're a police officer."

There was a moment of silence.

"But the fact remains, I'm winging it," Cecilia said in what was suddenly a very different tone of voice. "I'm just making it up as I go along."

"It seems to be working. Was capturing the tanks what you planned with the commander last night?"

"It was. But I've no idea what's supposed to happen next. Actually, I think I've already got one bit wrong—what I said about Kesselring massacring Italians. The real one certainly did massacre Italians, but I'm pretty sure it hasn't happened yet. I've charged him with something he's *going* to do."

"I dare say he deserves it anyway," Verity said.

"Well, yes. But how on earth are we to get out of this? I

mean—are we now to go through an alternate universe version of the whole of the rest of World War II?"

She walked to the window and gazed out. It was true she'd enjoyed arresting that Nazi general, even if it was only in a virtual reality.

But now?

THIRTY-THREE

The same, a few seconds later.

Cecilia stood for several minutes gazing out of the window at the piazza, which was gradually filling with people. She gave a big sigh.

"I really don't know…"

Again Verity experienced the strange shimmer that she had felt just before they met Andrea Cavaliere. This time it was accompanied by a change in the light, which suddenly became brighter, more golden.

"I think our friend Cecilia Anna Maria has already won the game." The voice came from behind her, and spoke with a slight German accent. "So now it is time to leave it."

Verity turned toward the voice and saw a man in a black cloak standing by the door. Medium height, dark hair touched with gray, dark-bearded, a little past his youth.

She glanced back at Cecilia, who still stood staring out of the window.

"Cecilia Anna Maria does not see me," the man said. "I was sent to her in the past, and to our dear Father Michael, and if you tell them about me, they will know who I am tell and I dare say they will tell you the story. But for now I am sent not to them but to you."

"And—forgive me, sir—who are you?"

"No, no, it is *I* who need to be forgiven! I frequently find the people I'm sent to so interesting that I forget to tell them who I am. My name is Friedrich Spee von Langenfeld, and I am a priest of the Society of Jesus—a Jesuit. I died in 1635."

"You *died*? But you're not a ghost!"

He laughed.

"No, my dear, I am not a ghost. I am alive in the Beloved, and I await the general resurrection, as do we all. And in the meantime I serve as I am sent. And just now I am sent to you."

"In a computer program? In a virtual reality?"

Again he laughed.

"In, but not of! *Si iacuero in inferno, ades! If I go down to hell, thou art there!* So do you really think that the servants of our Beloved cannot manage to get themselves into a computer program? Or virtual reality?"

"I suppose not. But then if Cecilia knows you, I dare say the computer could have created you out of her memories."

"Yet in her memories I was sent to her, whereas now I am sent to you."

Verity thought for a moment.

"So you aren't just in the computer program?" she said.

"Not *just* in the computer program, no."

She considered again.

"So—am I having a mystical experience?"

"If you mean by 'mystical' that you're in an altered state of consciousness, then no, you aren't. If you mean that my being with you makes you more aware of the presence of our Beloved, then yes, you are."

Verity gazed at him for a moment.

"I've never had much time for altered states of consciousness," she said finally. "I generally find enough to keep me busy in the state of consciousness I've already got."

Father Spee gazed back at her for a moment, his eyes filled with mischief.

"Oh, Verity, Verity! Truth by name, and by nature true as Toledo steel! You really *would* die defending the breach beside your comrade if you had to!"

"I hope I would, if I had to. But I'd much rather live."

He chuckled.

"Of course you would. And a very sensible choice! Especially since you and your friend Joseph have fallen in love. I rejoice for you both."

Verity had the odd feeling that she ought to be surprised by his knowing about her and Joseph, yet for some reason she wasn't.

So she merely said, "Thank you, Father. Some people seem to think we've been a bit slow."

"Then they know nothing of the matter. First friendship, then affection, and now *erōs*: yours has been a very fitting progress."

He smiled.

"But to business! — this program in which our friend Herbert Grieg has placed you. Cecilia Anna Maria has won the game, but it is not working as Herbert hoped. Some of his programming is good, but in other respects he actually has very little idea of what he is dealing with."

Verity nodded.

"That doesn't surprise me, Father. It's obvious he's remarkably clever in a lot of ways, but he doesn't actually *think* all that clearly. I know Cecilia's worried about this. She's brave, and she doesn't want to upset me by saying it, but I can see she's anxious, all the same."

"Of course she is anxious. She is far too intelligent not to be. And I see that you are anxious too."

"I am."

"Remember, then, in life or in death you are in the hands of our Beloved. Poor Herbert — in his delusion he looks to the *future* creation of an intelligence greater than human, and thinks that will change the universe. His maps are so small! If they were not, it might occur to him that the universe *already* contains intelligences greater than human, and always has—intelligences that his supercomputers will not match if they evolve for a million years! And the greatest of these, the loftiest archangels, delight to know that sustaining them is a divine *copia* even they can never plumb. And that *copia*, that inexhaustible and inestimable intelligence, is the source of those very values—right and wrong, justice, mercy, love—that poor Herbert thinks will so quickly be done for by his comical little *singularity*!"

"He also thinks he'll be able to achieve everlasting life."

Spee nodded.

"And perhaps his desire for that, however inchoate and ill informed, is a sign of hope for him. Perhaps he does have some awareness that what he has now is only a beginning."

"So that is good in him?"

"Yes… and no. Because this continuing existence that he and those like him actually propose, whether by constantly repairing their bodies or by downloading their minds into silicon— that existence, even if they achieved it, would not *be* everlasting life at all. If anything, it would be an *avoidance* of everlasting life, for it would simply prolong the life they already have. And that life, interesting and wonderful though it may be, is intended by our Beloved as no more than a prologue—prologue to a *new* creation in which past, present, and future are woven together in an eternal and ever evolving dance in which nothing that has been good or beautiful will ever be lost. As it is written, *'Surge qui dormis, et exsurge a mortuis, et illuminabit te Christus.'"*

He stopped, and smiled at her.

She found herself smiling back. *Awake, thou that sleepest, and arise from the dead, and Christ shall give thee light.*

"I've always loved that verse," she said. "It's full of hope."

"It is, and will be." He paused, then said, "But for this moment what matters is that our Beloved brings good out of folly, and something good has come out of this. Herbert sent you and Cecilia Anna Maria here for a foolish purpose, and our Beloved has used it for a better. Cecilia Anna Maria has spoken good words to her great uncle Andrea—words that strengthened that young man and gave him hope when he needed it."

"So that part of it *was* real?"

Spee smiled.

"A small loop in time was all that was required."

Verity nodded.

"I thought it seemed more real when it happened," she said.

"I know you did. And you were right. But now *you* need to get out of this program."

"So are you going to get us out, Father?"

He laughed.

"No, child! I was not sent to get you out but to encourage you—rather as our friend Cecilia Anna Maria encouraged Andrea. You do not *need* me to get you out. Verity, think what Joseph has taught you! Herbert's programming will not do it, but *you* know how to stop this program. *Think what you know!* That is what I was sent to tell you."

He looked again at Cecilia.

"Salute our beloved Cecilia Anna Maria for me and our beloved Father Michael. And her mother and father and the heroic Figaro! They are all my friends. Salute them all for me in the name of our Lord Jesus Christ."

He turned back to Verity.

"And when I have gone, *think about what you know.*"

"I will. And—and Father, thank you for what you said about Joseph and me. It isn't always easy, you know."

"I know."

"So may I… could I—it may seem a bit silly but would it be all right to give you a hug before you go?"

He smiled.

"Dear child, there is nothing silly about it and of course it would be all right! Do you think there are no hugs in heaven? One reason our Beloved gave us those wonderful, fragile things called bodies—for which, alas, our misguided friend Herbert has such contempt—is that they are so good for hugging."

Not knowing quite why she suddenly felt so free, Verity stepped up to him, put her arms around him, and stretching up kissed him on his cheek, which was warm and smooth above the soft down of his beard.

He looked down at her, smiling.

"Thank you, Verity, child of truth. I know that in the Beloved we shall meet again."

As she released him he stepped back, still smiling at her, turned on his heel, and was gone.

There was another shimmer, and the light returned to normal.

THIRTY-FOUR

The same, seconds later.

"... what we ought to do next," Cecilia said, completing her sentence and turning back to Verity.

There was a pause. Verity stared at her.

Cecilia frowned.

"Have I missed something?" she said.

"I'm afraid you've missed a quite a lot. You've been sort of switched off for the last five minutes or so. But your friend Father Spee — he was here."

"*Father Spee!* You saw him?"

"While you were looking out of the window. He said to salute you and Michael and everyone in the name of Our Lord Jesus Christ. And he said that Herbert Grieg's programming is no good for this bit, but that I know how to get us out."

"But that's wonderful! How?"

"I don't know."

"But I thought you said —"

"He said I know how to get us out but he didn't actually say *what* I know. He said to think about what Joseph's taught me. And then he left."

"He does tend to come and go a bit suddenly," Cecilia said, "and I know it can be disorienting."

"That's all right," Verity said. "I liked him. He knew all about me and Joseph and he was very nice about it." She sighed. "But what is it I know?"

Cecilia laughed. Somehow Verity's having seen Father Spee had lightened her spirits.

"There's no point in asking *me*. You're the one who knows it!"

Verity thought for a minute, then—

"Well, Father Spee seemed to think you'd already won the game. So maybe you should just say, 'End program,' like they do in *Star Trek* and *Deep Space Nine*."

"What do you mean?"

"Joseph's a trekker—we watch it a lot. In *Star Trek* and *Deep Space Nine*, when they're in the holodeck or one of those holo-suites, they'll be in the middle of some scene from history like we are, and then they have to leave for some reason, so they say 'Computer, end program,' and it all goes away."

"Go on, try it," Cecilia said.

"Computer, end program."

Nothing happened.

"Oh," Verity said, "it would have to be you, wouldn't it? After all, it's your program, your family history. And you're the one that's won the game. So you say it."

"Computer, end program," Cecilia said.

Nothing happened.

"Oh well," Verity said, "I guess that wasn't much of an idea."

"At least you've had an idea, which is more than I've managed so far."

"I wish Joseph was here. He'd know what to do."

"That's a thought! You said Father Spee told you to think about what Joseph has taught you. Well, let's imagine him. What do you think he'd say if he were here?"

Again Verity took a minute to think.

"Well, whenever we have a serious computer problem, Joseph always says we must start at the beginning."

"Which is?" Cecilia asked.

"What's the basis? What's the foundation of computer logic?"

"And what *is* the foundation of computer logic?"

"It's a binary system," Verity said.

"Which means what, exactly?"

"When Joseph's having a bad day he says it means computers are idiots whose only virtue is that they can count up to two extremely fast."

"And on a good day?"

"On a good day it means computers have a logic system that deals with any question by giving the answer yes or no."

"But does that apply here? Isn't this some sort of super computer?"

Verity shrugged.

"It's still a computer. The basic principles apply."

Cecilia nodded and waited.

Verity considered.

"So..." she said, "we need to stop the program."

"Yes."

"Right... and one infallible way to do that is, of course, to make the system crash."

"Can we do that?"

"I don't know that anyone's tried it from inside before. But since the program reacts to us—I mean, if you call your adjutant, he answers—I suppose we must be feeding the computer with some information from where we are, and it must be paying some attention to us. So there might be a way."

Cecilia waited.

After a moment or so, Verity spoke again, slowly and carefully.

"Joseph says that when a binary system receives two similar but not quite identical pieces of information, at nearly but not exactly the same time, it may vacillate."

"Meaning?"

"Meaning that instead of saying 'yes' or 'no,' it says, '*I don't know.*' And that's a glitch. It can't really do that. So the system crashes. You have to reboot."

"Could we do that? Give it this tricky information?"

"Maybe."

Verity paused, and again Cecilia waited.

At last Verity said, "What if we tried something again with the 'Computer end program' idea? I think probably we were right to address the computer directly."

"But it didn't work.'

"I think I know why. Very probably it's been told not to accept commands from unauthorized persons, or without the right password, or something."

"That makes sense."

"But suppose you were to say, '*Computer, I'd like you to end this program when Verity tells you to.*' And suppose I came in as you were halfway through and said, '*Computer, Cecilia would like you to end this program as she just told you to.*' Now those are strictly speaking statements, not commands, so that might get us past that barrier. And as statements, though they aren't incompatible, they're not exactly the same, either. So we just might make it wonder what the double input meant and hesitate — which is all we need."

"It would crash?"

"It might."

"And that could get us out of the program?"

"It could."

"Let's try it, then."

"Ma'am — when computers crash, data gets corrupted. It happens all the time. So even if this works, I don't know what it will do to us. On his own evidence, everyone else who's been in Grieg's program so far has come out of it either dead or bonkers."

"Verity," Cecilia said softly, "dearest friend, I know."

She reached out and took Verity's hand.

"But we do have to do something," she said. "Can you think of anything else to try?"

"No, ma'am."

"And certainly I can't. At least this way we're trying to do what Father Spee told you to do. And he's not let me down yet."

She took Verity's other hand, so that they stood facing each other.

"So," she said, "I'm to come in first, right?"

"Yes, ma'am."

"Here we go. *Computer, I'd like you to end this program when Verity tells you to.*"

As Cecilia said "when," Verity chimed in with "*Computer, Cecilia would like you to end this program as she just told you to.*"

The lights went out.

THIRTY-FIVE

Saint Mary's Rectory, 11:45 p.m.

Michael dried his hands on a tea towel and surveyed the kitchen. The dishwasher was empty. The clean dishes and utensils were back in the cupboards and drawers where they belonged. There was fresh water in the bowl by the sink for creatures who became thirsty during the night. Mama had tended to Cecilia's plants.

Rachel, thank God, was asleep in her room.

Figaro had had his last walk of the day and was now asleep in his usual place beside Rachel's cot.

Mama and Papa had gone to bed.

Felix and Marlene had departed on some mysterious feline business of the night.

In short, everyone was where he or she ought to be.

Well, nearly everyone.

He sat up late and watched television: four politicians arguing about Scottish independence. After listening to them for about fifteen minutes he came to three conclusions. First, he didn't give a damn. Second, he couldn't for the life of him see why anyone else did. Third, he had no idea why he was watching this twaddle anyway.

He switched off the television.

To be embraced by a silence that ought to have been broken by the telephone ringing and someone telling him that Cecilia was all right and her being out of communication for several hours had been merely a matter of... of... whatever it was that had kept her out of communication for several hours.

That, of course, was why he'd switched on the television and watched that ridiculous program in the first place. He was generally bored by politicians and disliked political broadcasts. But he disliked this silence even more—this particular silence in which the telephone did *not* ring and someone did *not* tell him that Cecilia was all right.

He looked at the clock.

It was time to say compline and go to bed.

THIRTY-SIX

Cecilia found herself lying on what seemed to be a bed in a darkened room. The mattress was firm and not uncomfortable. After a second or two she realized that there was some light from dim bulbs in the ceiling and thus lay still, waiting until her eyes adjusted to it.

"Are you there, ma'am?" Verity's voice was soft and cautious.

"Yes. And I think you've done it, Verity. You got us out. Good for you!"

She sat up.

There were wires attached to her head by little suction pads—so at least Grieg had told the truth about the connections to the computer not being invasive. She pulled them off. As her vision adjusted she could see Verity opposite her, also pulling off wires.

And now a red light was blinking on the A.D.A.M.1 console.

She swung her feet onto the ground and then, cautiously, stood up. She flexed her fingers and, again cautiously, took a step. She felt somewhat disoriented, but otherwise everything seemed to be working. Opposite her, Verity also got slowly to her feet.

They were in the room like a hospital ward they had seen earlier. And the figures on the other beds were starting to stir.

"Is this our next problem?" Verity said, looking at them.

"It could be our next opportunity."

She and Verity had been speaking softly, and now, as the first of the Africans sat up and stared at her, with her left hand she made a dramatic gesture towards the door and at the same time with her right put a finger to her lips. The African grinned broadly, his teeth gleaming white and strong in the near darkness. He placed his own finger on his lips, then turned to his fellows to give them the same message as they regained consciousness.

Cecilia looked at the door. The lock was a push-button combination.

"Top two then bottom two," Verity said quietly.

"How do you know?"

"Grieg thought I was out of it by the time he left, so he didn't worry about hiding what he was doing. But I'd just managed to hang on and I saw."

"Oh fabulous woman!"

Cecilia went to the door, pressed the buttons in the order Verity had given her, and opened the door cautiously a few inches. Well made and new, it made no sound.

The security guard was seated with his back to her. That was the good news.

The bad news was that he was already on the phone.

"The lights for ADAM1 are flashing here on the desk, sir," he said in his heavily accented English. "That means that some of the subjects are conscious, I think? Or perhaps the program is crashed?"

"It could be either or both."

That was Grieg's voice—she could hear what he said over the desk intercom quite clearly.

"Whatever you do," Grieg continued, "keep the door locked. We'll be there in a few minutes."

"Yes, sir."

Cecilia waited until the security guard had replaced the phone and was again peering at the console. She then opened the door and was upon him before he realized what was happening.

"Up!" she said softly, gripping him by his arm and twisting it hard. "I'll break your arm and probably several other bits of you if you give me any trouble. Into the ward! Now!"

Grunting with pain, he complied.

"Tie him up. Use the cables." She pointed to the wires that had connected them to the computer.

The Africans seized him eagerly.

She looked closely at the African she'd spoken to first. Strong, aquiline features —

"Wait a minute! I recognize you — from the battle for Rome — but how's that possible?"

"We were your Italian Africa police, ma'am. All of us! That's where you saw me. Yoruba, at your service ma'am. Everyone else in the program seemed to think you two were men. But we all knew."

"But that was a program based on DCI Cavaliere's memories," Verity said. "How on earth did all of you get into it? Shouldn't the computer have come up with something for you based on your memories?"

"I don't know, ma'am. After they brought us here that fellow Grieg told us he was programming computers in a way no one had ever been clever enough to do before, and we were going to find ourselves in a story about Africa that he'd program for us, and we should think ourselves lucky to be part of his great experiment. And then a doctor in a white coat came and injected us with something. After that I think I was in a story about Africa for a bit, although I can't remember it very clearly — but then I found myself with the others and we realized we'd switched to another story that wasn't about Africa at all but about Italy in World War II, and we were Italian African police. Perhaps Grieg isn't as clever as he thinks he is."

Verity nodded.

"Clearly he isn't. The relationship between his programs and the people he links to them seems completely haphazard."

"I doubt it's completely haphazard, ma'am, but whatever principles lie behind it, obviously he doesn't properly understand them."

"Yes," Verity said, "that's much better put. I'm sure you're right."

"Well," Cecilia said, "whoever we all were back there, here and now I'm DCI Cecilia Cavaliere of Exeter CID, this is DS Verity Jones, and we're very pleased to meet you. And fascinating though this conversation is, right now we need to get organized. Grieg knows we're awake and he's on his way."

THIRTY-SEVEN

The U.N.I.T.E.D. tower, a few minutes later.

G rieg, excited and curious about the news Jansons had given him, barely took time to gather a couple more security guards before going to the elevator.

"The subjects of the experiment may be in a subdued state," he told them, "or they may be violent. We've no idea. Be prepared to kill them if necessary. In any case we shall have to kill them all afterwards. But it will be good to get as much information from them as we can first, so let's not kill them *before* it's necessary."

"Yes, sir."

What he was not prepared for was the sight that greeted him when the lift doors opened. The dark-haired policewoman was seated facing him with her feet on Jansons's desk and a broad grin on her face. The other, the little blonde, was standing beside her, smiling sweetly.

"What the hell's going on!" he shouted. "Jansons, where the hell are you? Get away from that desk, you bitches!"

He strode into the room, the two security guards following behind him.

The little blonde, still smiling sweetly, turned away from him momentarily while he was yelling at her, then pivoted towards him as he came within her reach — launching a straight right-hand punch that took him squarely on the jaw, somewhat off balance, and utterly by surprise. Caught off balance he saw stars, reeled backward, and hit the floor with a jarring thud that knocked him for an instant witless and breathless.

"*That,*" the no-longer-sweetly-smiling blonde said, looking down at him, "is for saying I was *partially* educated."

The boss-lady now swung her feet off the desk and stood up, covering him with Jansons's MP5. From her manner of handling the semi-automatic weapon it was clear she knew quite well how to use it.

"Now, Verity," she said, without taking her eyes off him, "you shouldn't mock your enemy when he's down. It's not sporting. As for Jansons, Mr. Grieg, I'm afraid he can't help you. He's rather tied up at the moment."

THIRTY-EIGHT

The same. A few minutes later.

Despite the seriousness of the situation, Cecilia found it hard not to laugh at the expression on Grieg's face as Verity hit him and he went down. Verity might be small, but she knew how to throw a punch, and every kilogram she had was behind it.

And Yoruba and his colleagues, who had been lurking out of sight on each side of the lift doors when they opened, had stepped out behind the two security guards as they followed Grieg into the room and gently but firmly pinioned and disarmed them.

Grieg looked as though he were trying to rise.

"No, don't get up," Cecilia said. "Stay where you are. Put your hands on your head where I can see them. You two as well. Hands on your head and down on your knees. Now lie down on your front, face toward the floor. Hands still on your heads! All three of you. Yes, I know it's awkward. Actually, it's meant to be. Do it, or you'll have bullet wounds in very painful places, which you'll find even more awkward. And *if* you know anything about anything, Mr. Grieg, which I confess I'm beginning to doubt, you'll know the boss detective lady means what she's saying."

The two security guards did as they were told.

So did Grieg.

"You'll be sorry for this," he muttered with difficulty from the floor.

"Who knows? One day perhaps I will, Mr. Grieg. But not at the moment! At the moment you're out of luck."

"Screw you both!"

"I'm afraid you're out of luck there, too. I'm already taken and so is Detective Sergeant Jones."

"I *thought*," Detective Sergeant Jones said to no one in particular, "we were not to mock our enemies when they were down on the floor."

"Ah yes, quite right," Cecilia said. "That *is* the general rule for detective sergeants. Obviously, it does not apply to detective chief inspectors."

"Oh well, that's all right then," Verity said. "I just wondered."

Cecilia turned to one of the Africans who was not carrying a gun.

"I'm afraid, sir, I don't know your name."

"Kamau, ma'am."

"Well then, Kamau, would you mind fetching some more of the cables from the ward? There are plenty of them. We can truss these fellows too."

"That will be a pleasure!"

She turned to one of the Africans who had taken a gun.

He grinned.

"I am N'kosi, ma'am," he said, before she could ask him.

"Thank you. N'kosi." She pointed to the MP5. "You look as if you know how to use that thing."

"Alas, ma'am, yes. Better than I wish to. I think I am what you call a good shot."

Cecilia nodded.

"All right. And you, Yoruba?" He had taken the other MP5.

"I've used one of these before, ma'am.

"Good. Now we need to cover the lift door. Someone else

may come. Grieg may have sent for the doctor fellow—Telfer. Yoruba, you and I can cover these three and the lift."

Kamau returned swiftly, and within minutes they had Grieg and the two security guards trussed and helpless.

"Ma'am, why don't we immobilize the lift too, just for the present? All we need do is jam the doors open."

"Good idea, Verity. Go for it."

But Kamau, with the other two, whose names were Kitemo and Gatura, was already manhandling chairs between the open doors.

"We need to cover the other door, too, the door to the ward. I dare say there's another way up. I'm hoping the rest of Grieg's minions haven't realized anything's wrong yet, but they may at any moment. N'kosi, are you good for that?"

"I shall do it, ma'am."

"Excellent. We seem to be secure for the present. It's time, I think, to use that phone, if it's still operating."

Verity peered at it again.

"It says, 'Dial 0 to ask for outside line.' Shall I try it?"

"Yes. Try to make your voice sound like a man's."

"Why do that?"

"They'll be more used to taking orders from men."

"For heavens' sake, ma'am, this is the twenty-first century—"

"Verity, are you trying to raise their consciousness or get us out of here?"

"Oh! Yes, of course! Right, ma'am."

Verity pressed the "0" button.

When the operator answered, she said, "Could you get me an outside line, please?"

"That sounded to me just the same as your usual voice only a bit lower," Cecilia said.

"Yes, sir," the operator said.

Verity smirked.

A moment later the dial tone was audible. Verity stabbed in

a number for Edgestow police, and as it started to ring passed the handset to Cecilia.

THIRTY-NINE

The same. A moment later.

"Sergeant Wyatt!"

"DCI Cavaliere! Am I glad to hear you, ma'am! Are you and DS Jones all right?"

"Yes we are, sort of. But we've got a bit of a situation on our hands. We're inside the institute, and there's some very strange business going on. For starters they kidnapped us. At the moment we've escaped and we're okay, but any minute now they may realize that we've taken some of their lot prisoner and are holed up here, and then all hell could break loose. How fast can you get some people out here?"

"All in hand, ma'am. They should be there any minute now."

"Any *minute*? How on earth—"

"Joseph realized there was a problem this morning, ma'am. It was him that alerted the rest of us. To cut a long story short, the chief super's on his way and he's got a search warrant, so they can't keep him out."

"There are a lot of semi-automatic weapons floating around here. He may meet some resistance."

"Yes, ma'am, he knows. He's bringing armed officers in case of trouble."

"Are you in touch with him now?"

"I can be, ma'am.'

"Well, Sergeant, can you tell him that we're in the tower? And there's a secret to the tower. It looks as if it's got twenty floors — that's how many buttons there are in the lift. But there's an extra floor between the nineteenth and twentieth, and *that's* the floor where we're holed up. To get to us in the lift, you have to press the buttons for nineteen and twenty simultaneously and hold them down for several seconds. That makes the lift stop at the extra floor."

"I'll tell him, ma'am."

"Good. Sergeant, let's keep this line open if we can, or at least as long as we can. Then you can hear us and you can tell us what's going on."

"Yes ma'am. I'll talk to the chief super now. Just give me a minute."

She put the handset down onto the desk, careful not to hang up, and looked at the bound figures on the floor.

"Well," she said, "it's starting to look as if our Sergeant Wyatt and his friends just might be somewhat sharper knives than you thought, Mr. Grieg."

"How on earth do *you* know all that stuff about the extra floor?" Verity asked.

"There's a click every time the lift passes a floor," Cecilia said. "Only I noticed when we came up the first time that between the nineteenth and the twentieth there was an extra click. That was the first thing that set me wondering about this place. But then when Grieg brought us back here after he'd pulled his guns on us, I managed to watch out of the corner of my eye what he did in the lift. And I saw what buttons he pressed."

"DCI Cavaliere! Are you there?" Sergeant's Wyatt's voice came from the phone, and she returned her attention to it.

"Here, Sergeant."

"Chief Superintendent Davies and his people are already in position by the institute's gate ma'am. He's says to tell you he's coming in now. And he's got your message about the tower."

"Thank you, Sergeant. That's totally splendid."

She turned back to the others.

"Let's unjam the lift in five minutes," she said. "The cavalry are on their way."

FORTY

Susanna's farmer friend in the Laurels pub was right. Most of the Latvian security guards were indeed "decent enough lads." Despite toting Heckler and Koch MP5s, their training and their attitudes to what they were doing were not very different from the training and attitudes of the average British security officer.

There were, however, nine exceptions. Nine of the Eglītis security men reported directly to Herbert Grieg. These nine alone knew what was happening at the top of the U.N.I.T.E.D. tower. They had been extensively involved in the seizing and imprisonment of the African immigrants, just as they had participated this morning in the seizure of the two police officers. Their leader, thanks to Grieg's appointment and by his own inclination, was Markuss Ozols.

Markuss Ozols enjoyed his gun and his uniform, in fact could think of no better way to live than to fight and no better way to die than in battle. Perhaps he was born out of his time. In the age of Genghis Khan he might have been a hero. In World War II he might have found a certain satisfaction, as had his grandfather Aleksis, who served in the 19th Waffen Grenadier Division. The division surrendered to the Red Army on 9th May 1945, among the very last of Nazi Germany's military to do so.

His grandson Markuss inherited from Aleksis a violent hatred of Russians and an equally violent hatred of the western powers that cooperated with them in World War II. That evolved into hatred of what the new Latvia became, as it escaped from the claws of the Soviets only to become another western nation and a prosperous capitalist economy in a democratic Europe. Markuss loathed the bourgeois peace of his country with an almost perfect hatred. He lacked sufficient discipline to be in the military in a time of peace, but he was an enthusiastic security guard. He could carry a weapon and wear a uniform and even occasionally shout at people and perhaps get to shoot them, all without the tedium of military discipline.

It was Markuss who realized that something was wrong in the U.N.I.T.E.D. tower. A nose for trouble led him to call Jansons on the nineteenth-plus floor.

The line was busy.

After a few minutes he tried again.

Still busy.

He checked with the operator.

"The line's in use," she said after a few minutes.

"Who by?"

"I'm not sure, sir."

"Patch me in. Let me hear."

"Sir, I'm not sure I should — "

"This may be important, woman. Patch me in!"

"Yes, sir."

Ozols was in time to hear the last of Cecilia's words to Sergeant Wyatt.

He drew his own conclusions.

A less dedicated man might have decided that if the forces of law and order were about to descend upon them, it was time to get out. Not so Markuss Ozols. He summoned his five remaining colleagues, who were playing cards and watching television in their quarters on the tenth floor.

"Those police bitches and the blacks have broken loose. I think they've taken Mr. Grieg and the others prisoner. They're on the extra floor. They'll be watching the main lift, but we can take them out from the back stairs. You tackle them from the rear door to the ward where the prisoners were, and while you keep them occupied with that I'll go round by the outside ledge and give them a little surprise through the main office windows. Let's go and blow their fucking heads off."

The five seized their MP5s and mounted the stairs.

FORTY-ONE

Edgestow. Near the entrance to U.N.I.T.E.D. 1:55 a.m.

Chief Superintendent Davies checked the time, then spoke into his mobile.

"Listen up, people. We go in at 0200 hours as planned. Units check in and confirm you're in position and ready to go."

The various units — three vans and three cars for back up — responded in order.

"Good. Then on my mark."

Davies nodded to the van driver, who switched on the engine and the headlights, pulled out from the side of the road, then almost immediately turned right into the institute gateway. Facing them was a weighted barrier and to their right a lighted window for the controller, an Eglītis security guard in his dark gray uniform.

"I am Chief Superintendent Glyn Davies of Exeter CID," Davies called out, "and I have a warrant to search these premises. Raise the barrier at once, please."

"This is a United Nations property," the security guard said, speaking with something of a mid-European accent. "A local magistrates' warrant cannot admit you here. I suggest — "

"Sorry, son," Davies said, "that won't fly. Now I'm asking you nicely for the last time. Raise the barrier at once, if you please."

"This is United Nations prop—"

Davies turned and nodded to the members of the Armed Response Unit who were seated in the back of the van. Without a word they opened the rear doors. Two of them ran to the barrier and began raising it while two more went to the hut, where the security guard was already picking up the phone.

"That's all right, sir," one of them said, taking it from him, "no need to announce us. We'll announce ourselves. We're good at that. And in the meantime you're under arrest for obstructing the police."

Back in the van, Davies's driver waited only until the barrier had been raised and the security man was being led to one of the other waiting police cars, then grinned and put his foot down.

The van proceeded on its way at a fair speed, followed by a second and a third. The rough road caused a good bit of jolting and bouncing, but the drivers knew their business, nothing worse occurred, and some minutes later the vans came to a halt at the tower. The armed police spilled out onto the tarmac.

"We follow standard procedure," Davies said.

"Sir!"

FORTY-TWO

The same, a few minutes later.

N'kosi was watching the rear door to the ward. He saw when the first Eglītis security man appeared in his dark gray uniform, and the Eglītis man saw him. Each fired at the other, but as both were at the same time diving for cover, neither shot hit its mark.

"The security guards are here!" N'kosi shouted over his shoulder to Cecilia and the others. "They're using their guns. But I have the door covered."

The impasse lasted several minutes.

First one, then another of the guards darted around the door to the ward and let off a shot, but none of them had time to take proper aim, and N'kosi was not to be caught out. He fired back every time, avoided damage himself, and at least once, to judge by the pained yelp, succeeded in wounding one of his assailants.

And now Cecilia faced the kind of problem that confronts every commander with limited resources and the possibility of being assailed on two fronts: she did not want to leave N'kosi unsupported *and* she wanted to keep covering the entrance to the lift, in case not the police but more of Grieg's men came that way.

"N'kosi, can you manage for a bit?" she shouted.

"Easy!" he shouted back. "We have much better fighters than these in Africa. And I told you—I am a good shot!"

Cecilia smiled.

"Yoruba," she said, "can you watch the lift for a bit while I see if I can give N'kosi some support?"

"Yes, General!" he said. "We are all fighting together. It will be just like la Magliana!"

They both laughed.

Cecilia was still laughing as she saw a gray-uniformed figure with a gun loom at them suddenly out of the darkness beyond the office windows and fire at her.

Yoruba must have seen too, for he threw himself into the path of the bullets, taking them in his chest. They spun him around and he crumpled.

Cecilia flung herself sideways and at the same time brought up her own weapon, firing back over Yoruba's falling body. The gray gunman's weapon flew into the air. He reeled back and disappeared into the darkness.

Cecilia looked down at Yoruba, whose chest was already a mass of blood.

"Oh dear God," she said.

And now Verity was beside her.

"Give me the gun, ma'am," she said. "I'll cover the lift and the windows for you."

It was a lot for her to cover, but Cecilia handed her the weapon and knelt beside Yoruba, cradling him in her arms.

"Yoruba, you took that for me," she said.

He smiled up at her.

"For my general," he said. "That makes me... African and Roman... as you said... yes?"

"It makes you a splendid African and a splendid Roman, Yoruba. The legions would have been honored to have you."

He gave her another smile.

"We have... defended Rome... my general!"

His head slumped, his eyes closed.

She felt for his pulse.

There was none.

"Damn!" she said.

She could feel the tears starting into her eyes.

"Damn! Damn! Damn! What a total bloody waste of a beautiful man!"

"I don't think he thought that, ma'am," Verity said, not taking her eyes off the window and the lift. "And I don't either," she added. "Do you want the gun back?"

But Cecilia thought it almost certain that she had just killed a man.

And she knew for sure that she was angry.

Very angry.

It was surely better that Verity — calm, rational Verity — had the gun now.

"You hang on to it," she said.

Twenty-one floors below, Glyn Davies strode through the large glass doors that provided the main entrance to the tower, and to the utter surprise of the few late night personnel on duty in the atrium announced himself in a loud voice.

"I am Chief Superintendent Glyn Davies of the Exeter CID. This is a police operation and I have a warrant to search these premises. Stay exactly where you are."

As he was speaking, officers of the Armed Response Unit were already coming quickly and quietly through the doors on either side of him.

"Alpha unit, the lift. You know what to do. Bravo unit find the emergency stairway. Secure it and take control of the adjoining floors. Go!"

"Sir!"

FORTY-THREE

The U.N.I.T.E.D. tower. A few minutes later.

"Ma'am," Verity said with a nod towards the lift doors. The lights were blinking. The lift was on the move.

"Let's hope it's the cavalry. But get to the side, Verity, in case it isn't."

They positioned themselves and waited, Verity holding the MP5 steady and unwavering.

Until, after a few seconds, the doors opened, and the burly figures of armed police in flack jackets and helmets spilled into the room.

The lead man surveyed the scene of devastation, from Yoruba's still, crumpled figure to the prone, trussed figures of the two security guards and Grieg. He turned to the two women.

"Detective Chief Inspector Cecilia Cavaliere, I take it. And Detective Sergeant Verity Jones."

"Yes," Cecilia said. "That's us."

"And are we glad to see you," Verity added.

A couple of shots sounded from the ward.

"That's N'kosi," Cecilia said. "Be careful, he's on our side. He's been holding off the enemy for us. All right N'kosi!" she shouted. "Our people are here. They're coming in behind you."

"Yes, ma'am!" N'kosi shouted. "I've still got it covered!"

He rather sounded as if he were enjoying himself.

The situation was soon resolved.

The second unit of armed police came up the emergency stairs and the remaining security men, with nowhere to go, lay down their weapons and were taken into custody.

N'kosi was unscathed, but two of the security men were wounded.

Clearly, N'kosi was a *very* good shot.

FORTY-FOUR

The U.N.I.T.E.D. Tower, the ground floor.
Fifteen or so minutes later.

"We nearly got away with it, you know," Grieg said as they put the handcuffs on him. "It was only luck you got onto us."

Now where had she heard that before? Cecilia wondered as Grieg — of course! — continued talking.

"If it hadn't been for that asshole Frasier programming our address into his GPS system and then getting himself into that pile-up on the interstate or whatever you call it, you'd never have gotten onto us."

"Well, Mr. Grieg," Chief Superintendent Davies said, coming up to them just in time to hear this, "let us hope that these profound thoughts will be a great consolation to you during your years in prison."

He nodded to the two constables, who took Grieg away.

Davies looked around the room. Activity everywhere. Desks and cupboards were being searched. Computers and boxes of files and papers were being carried out.

He turned to Cecilia and Verity.

"Your friend Joseph started investigating their computers on line as soon as we got the search warrant — he penetrated their

systems in twenty minutes! He's that good. The one thing puzzling him is that there seems to be a lot of traffic about something that's happening tomorrow. Which I'm afraid rather suggests we're still not out of the woods. But it's encrypted and he
hasn't worked out what it is yet. He's on it, though—and he's
got a couple of his pals from the Europol Cybercrime Centre
helping. He says they'll work all night if they have to. He'll get
there. As for all this"—he waved to take in the action around
them—"there's obviously an enormous amount for us to check
out here."

"What about the other one, sir—Louis Cartwright?" Cecilia
asked.

"Ah, yes, the smooth and aristocratic Mr. Cartwright. Well,
you'll be happy to know that his aristocratic backside should
be being plucked from its aristocratic bed in the family man-
sion"—he glanced at a clock on the wall—"just about now. He
had no kind of criminal record—squeaky clean, so far as any of
us knew, and he was a figurehead, of course, even here—but
he was clearly complicit in what Grieg did to you. So I dare say
he's likely to be off the streets for a bit too."

"Does Sir James Harlow know about all this? It seems to me
he ought to."

"He's in Paris. The chief constable phoned him there at his
hotel. He was furious, of course, when he found out what had
been going on behind his back, and shocked to learn about
Cartwright. Apparently they've been friends for years—they
were together at Oxford—so it's a personal blow for him.
Anyway, he intends to be back here tomorrow afternoon to
take charge, which is the earliest he can manage. He says he has
something on that he must deal with in the morning. But it's
a relief to know he'll be back in the director's seat tomorrow,
even if it isn't until the afternoon."

"Yes, it is."

"Oh—and of course, among those we've arrested there's the
one you winged."

"Winged? Who did I wing?"

"The security guard on the ledge—the one who shot the African through the window. He was damned lucky. Your return shot grazed his head and knocked him out and he fell back onto the ledge. We fished him off it, and he'll recover. He could quite well have fallen *off* the ledge and dropped twenty floors. But then of course we're charging him with assault with a deadly weapon and with murder. So maybe he won't think he's so lucky after all."

With all that had happened, she had actually forgotten about that shot—the horror of which came flooding back to her now, mercifully alleviated by knowing now that she had not in fact killed the man.

His faults lie open to the laws; let them,
Not you, correct him.

Shakespeare as usual had got it right—although someone had told her recently that it wasn't Shakespeare at all but some other Elizabethan dramatist who wrote that bit. She still thought it was pretty good.

"Under the circumstances it was a rather brilliant shot," Verity said.

"Under the circumstances it was a damned lucky shot," she said—and meant it, in more ways than one. "But what about the other Africans?" she said. "N'kosi and Kamau and the other two? I know they're illegal immigrants, but those five saved our bacon. This all would have been a hell of a lot messier if it hadn't been for them."

"I promise you," Davies said, "all that's going to stand them in *very* good stead when their cases come up before immigration. The chief constable has already said he intends to speak on their behalf, and so will I."

"And the body of Yoruba? He gave his life to save mine."

"Of course we're treating him with respect. He was wearing a cross, so I take it he's a Christian and would want a Christian burial. That's all we know so far."

At which point the chief superintendent took a call on his mobile. Unless Cecilia quite misread his body language, he didn't like what he was hearing.

"Well then, there's nothing else we can do for the moment," he said. "Post a couple of officers at the house in case he comes back, and the rest of you'd better join us here. There's plenty to do."

He looked at Cecilia and Verity.

"Louis Cartwright's done a bunk. The officers I sent failed to find him." He paused. "Now, is there anything else?"

"It occurs to me, sir," Cecilia said, "that this fellow Teflon, the one the MI5 advisement was about, if he *was* going to do something around here—say, rob some banks in Exeter—this would be like the first part of his MO, wouldn't it?"

She gestured at all the activity around them.

"I mean, I know this isn't a massive disruption like having all the traffic lights go out or an underground railway break down, but it's having the same effect—lots of police tied up here. And if so, then maybe what Joseph Stirrup's onto—the 'something that's happening tomorrow'—could be the second part. If we knew what it was. It's just a thought."

But it was a thought that had clearly caught the chief superintendent's attention.

He frowned.

"But then," he said, "they couldn't have planned that pile-up on the M5 last week. Nobody could. And that would be an essential part of it. If it hadn't been for that you wouldn't have come here in the first place."

"Perhaps they didn't plan it. Perhaps it just happened and then somebody—maybe Cartwright—decided to take advantage of it. Leaving Grieg to be the fall guy."

The chief superintendent stared at her.

"In which case," he said slowly, "the elusive and until now

squeaky clean Louis Cartwright might be a lot cleverer than we thought. He might even be..."

Cecilia nodded.

"Yes, sir. That's what I was thinking. He might be Teflon."

FORTY-FIVE

Saint Mary's Rectory, Exeter. Friday, 30th August. 2:45 a.m.

The bedside telephone rang.

Michael, who had been dozing in uneasy catnaps, jerked himself into consciousness, reached over, and snatched the handset from its cradle, fumbling in his haste and barely managing not to drop it.

"Saint Mary's Rectory," he said, sitting up.

"Hello, darling, it's me."

"Oh Cecilia my love, thank God. Are you all right?"

"Yes I am. Verity and I've had a bit of an adventure. Long story for later and it's not over yet. But I'm fine. We're both fine."

"That's all I need to know."

They talked a little longer, she sent love to Rachel and her parents, they exchanged their own pledges and goodnights, and Michael replaced the handset.

He lay back on the pillow and sighed heavily with relief. The tight feeling had disappeared from the pit of his stomach.

He lay thus for several minutes, simply enjoying the fact that he wasn't feeling anxious. Then he decided he would get up and look in on Rachel.

In the corridor Felix and Marlene, tails upright like masts, emerged from the shadows and writhed ecstatically around his ankles, purring loudly. He bent and stroked them for a moment. Then they disappeared again, back into the shadows.

Catlike.

He shook his head.

Of course they were catlike.

They were cats.

He entered Rachel's room to a soft, welcoming thump from Figaro.

"Good boy, Fig," he whispered.

But Rachel was already awake. Two large brown eyes — already, it seemed to him, she had Cecilia's eyes — were gazing up at him.

"Hello Daddy," she said.

"Hello, sweetheart. I just talked to Mama on the phone. She sends you lots and lots of love."

Rachel smiled. Just as she had surely sensed earlier that something was wrong, so now she surely sensed his relief.

She reached up for him.

As he bent down to her it occurred to him, not for the first time, how extraordinarily blessed he was to have two sets of arms in the world in which he could feel such joy.

Figaro thumped again, this time more firmly, then stood up, shook vigorously, and came over to the cot, tail waving. Evidently Figaro too, having in his own way known earlier that something was wrong, now perceived the relief.

After a while Michael gently unclasped the little arms from around his neck, adjusted Rachel's covers, and kissed her forehead.

In the act of doing this he was moved suddenly, intensely, by a feeling for the harmony of all things — *musica universalis,* the music of the spheres. He and Cecilia had heard that music together once, and the recollection was almost painful — yet if it were pain it was a pain that exhilarated and entranced him, a pain he would not be without.

Beloved, already we are children of God, and it is not yet revealed what we shall be.

He sighed.

"Good night, little sweetheart," he said to his daughter.

But already she was asleep.

"Good boy," he said again to Figaro, scratching him where he liked to be scratched, behind his ears.

Figaro rubbed against him for a minute, then returned to his usual place, revolved several times, and curled up into his usual position with a comfortable grunt.

As Michael was emerging from Rachel's room, Andrea emerged from his and Rosina's.

"I'm afraid I must have woken you," Michael said softly.

"We did hear you," Andrea said, also softly, "but that was only because we weren't asleep anyway. And I thought I heard the telephone."

"You did. It was Cecilia—she's all right! I don't know the details yet—she says long story for later. But she's fine and sends her love."

"Thank God."

"Amen."

"I'll go and tell Rosina. I dare say we'll sleep now. Good night, Michael."

"Good night, Andrea."

Back in his and Cecilia's room, Michael got into bed.

"Thank you, Lord," he said as his head touched the pillow.

He might have said more, had he not fallen at once into a sweet, dreamless sleep.

FORTY-SIX

Edgestow, the U.N.I.T.E.D. tower. 2:55 a.m.

"Find somewhere in the building where you can get a couple of hours' sleep and freshen up," Chief Superintendent Davies told his detectives, "and then I want you both back in Exeter. I'm not sure what's going down this morning, if anything, but for the next few hours I want my best officers on deck and at the center."

They made it to Exeter by a little after 6.30 a.m., but the call from Joseph that Davies was waiting for didn't come through until 9.05. Gathered round his desk were DCI Cavaliere, DS Jones, and several of his other officers.

"We've just cracked it, sir," Joseph said. "It's to be a bomb. A busload of school kids, a Bluebell Tours Coach, is coming from Bristol to Exeter. There's a massive bomb on board—at least 4000 kilograms."

They all looked at each other, and there were several sharp intakes of breath.

"The bus is scheduled to come up through Palace Gate and Deanery Cloister and then drop the kids off directly in front of the west end of the cathedral—the dean and chapter have given special permission. The plan is to detonate the bomb as the bus stops. With the kids still on board."

"Jesus Christ!" Davies said softly. It was more a prayer than an oath.

"Then five minutes after the explosion, separate groups are set up to rob three banks simultaneously — to be exact, HSBC in Cowick Street, Barclays in Bedford Street, and Lloyds in the High Street."

"Where's the bus now?" Davies asked.

"On the road. sir. It set off half an hour ago from Bristol."

"How are they detonating it?"

"Sir, there's a car following — a Volvo XC70. A Russian they call Vasily is driving it. He planted the bomb on the bus last night and he'll detonate it from the car. My Europol pals checked on Vasily for me. He's ex-FSB, the Federal Security Service — that's the new KGB — and apparently he's good at what he does, except they fired him because they couldn't trust him. Anyway, he's going to detonate the bomb when he decides it's the right time. And if he thinks they've been spotted, or we're on to them, he's going to detonate the bomb anyway — wherever they happen to be. Just to warn us not to mess with them, I suppose."

"How near to the bus must he be to do it?"

"If he's anywhere closer to it than two hundred and fifty meters, I think he could probably do it."

"Dear God," Davies said. "That's a hell of a long way."

At his urgent request the Eurocopter was scrambled, and within a few minutes its crew had spotted the tour bus on the motorway and the Volvo following. It was a fine, clear morning and the pictures patched through to Davies's office were excellent — they could see both vehicles clearly and even read the "Bluebell Tours" logo on the side of the tour bus.

"How long before they get to Exeter?"

"Given current traffic conditions and speeds, I'd say about eighty-five minutes."

"All right. Pull away, then. You know Vasily mustn't think we're on to him."

"Yes, sir."

Davies thought for a moment, then turned to his officers.

"We've got to get him to stop, but in such a way that he doesn't think it's us."

"Not a road block, then," Cecilia said.

"No. It has to be road *works*—just before he's due to leave the motorway. Not a uniform in sight. Looks like we've got just over an hour to set it up. Reduce traffic to a single lane—that's bound to cause gridlock. Then somehow or other we've got to get our Russian friend out of that car."

"Couldn't someone take a shot at him while he's *in* the car, sir? Just take him out?"

The chief superintendent gazed quizzically at DS Verity Jones, from whom had come this surprisingly bloodthirsty suggestion. Had she been watching too much television?

In any case, he shook his head.

"There'd be no clear target, DS Jones. Didn't you notice on the pictures from the chopper? That Volvo's got reflective glass all round. It's not legal, of course, but just now probably wouldn't be a good moment to pull him over for it."

FORTY-SEVEN

The M5, a mile or so north of Junction 29. 10:26 a.m.

"Good morning, Mr. Griffiths. This is Chief Superintendent Glyn Davies of Exeter CID. I believe you're on the M5 in a single line of traffic that's stopped by road works at the moment."

Emrys Griffiths gazed at the mobile on his dashboard. He'd been driving for Bluebell Tours for years, and nothing like this had ever happened. At first he'd thought Cerys back at the office must be pulling his leg, but she'd convinced him. This really was a police superintendent they'd patched through to him.

"Yes, sir. Everything's come to a complete stop."

"Now Mr. Griffiths, we need your help. It could hardly be more important."

"I'll do what I can, sir."

"Thank you, Mr. Griffiths. There's a road worker with a phone standing directly in front of your bus at the moment, isn't there?"

Emrys looked up. A man in a high visibility jacket and cap was standing in front of the bus holding a mobile phone. He met Emrys's eye and nodded.

"Yes, sir. I see him."

"Good. He's actually a police officer. Now, here's what's

going to happen, Mr. Griffiths. In a few minutes, the traffic in front of you will start to move forward. When there are about ten yards clear in front of you the officer will step aside and give you a nod to move forward too. You are to move on slowly for about ten yards, then stop. Can you do that?"

"Yes, sir. Of course I can."

The traffic had for some time been reduced to a single-lane crawl, but that was not especially unusual and Vasily was not worried by it. There were a lot of workmen about who didn't appear to be doing anything—but there was nothing especially unusual about that, either. The British seemed always to be gluing up their roads for road works at which no one appeared to be doing anything. The main thing was that the tour bus also was being delayed. He had it in clear view, and the mobile telephone that would detonate the device was within easy reach on the seat beside him. So everything was well under control.

The tour bus in front of him began to move slowly forward, and he reached to take the Volvo out of park.

At which point a white Range Rover Sport, new, expensive, and shiny, zipped past him, honking loudly, stereo blaring—its wing mirror must have been within inches of his—and squeezed itself with a squeal of tires into the gap that had briefly opened between him and the tour bus.

Vasily grunted with irritation.

He'd caught sight of the driver as he went by—young, blond, sunglasses, pale cream jacket and a fancy colored shirt. Some fucking rich kid who thought he owned the world and whose father had more money than sense. Vasily was briefly tempted to blow up the bus now, just to take the rich kid and his luxury passion wagon with it.

But of course he did no such thing.

Business was business.

He could still see the bus, and in this jam no one was going anywhere.

He deliberately made himself breathe slowly. It was crucial to stay calm and focused.

And stick to the plan.

"Well done, Mr. Griffiths. That went perfectly. Now the next bit will be a bit trickier — though nothing that's going to be a problem for an experienced driver like yourself, I'm sure."

"I'll do my best, sir."

"Good man. This is it, then. This time when the traffic in front of you moves off, we want you stay where you are. Wait for a real gap to open up. When the officer in front of you reckons there's enough clear road — three quarters of a mile at least — he's going to step aside again and give you a nod, and here's the thing. I want you to drive off immediately, *accelerating* as fast as you possibly can. Can you do that? Never mind even if it frightens the children a bit. It's vital that you put as much distance as possible between yourself and where you are now as fast as you can."

"Yes, sir. I think I can do that, sir."

"Excellent. Then wait for the officer's signal."

The tour bus began finally to move forward.

And about time, too.

Vasily was beginning to think it never would.

The wait had been unconscionable even by British standards. He took the Volvo out of park into drive, ready to go, and waited.

But now the Range Rover, for all its flashy overtaking, was being slow off the mark.

Oh, come *on*! What the hell was the silly little idiot waiting for? Had he stalled his stupid fucking car?

And that bus was already pulling away fast.

Someone in the line close behind honked. Shut the fuck up! Do you think you're the only one getting pissed off?

At which instant the Range Rover's reversing lights came on and it was hurtling back toward him—fast! It smashed into the front of the Volvo with a grinding crash that sent it flying backwards, at the same time jerking Vasily painfully forward into his seatbelt.

Shit! He scrambled for the mobile phone, which at the moment of impact had shot forward onto the floor. Where the hell was it? There it was. *Shitfuckdamn*! He couldn't get at it because of the fucking seatbelt. He unfastened the belt—now, where was the damned phone? There, he had it!

He threw open the car door and used every curse word he knew.

The bus was already way out of range.

And now, adding irritation to injury, the door to the Range Rover in front of him opened and the blond young man got out of it, now minus sunglasses, smiling affably.

"Terribly sorry, old boy! Completely my fault. Put the dashed thing into reverse instead of drive. Silly me! I'll pay for the damage, of course."

Vasily swore again.

The bus was disappearing. He *must* catch it. And there was no way he could move the Volvo.

There was only one thing to do.

He punched the young man's jaw hard enough to knock him down, then sprinted to the Range Rover and leapt into it.

As the Range Rover started to move, the young man came gracefully to his feet and produced a Glock 17 semi-automatic pistol from under his jacket.

Swiftly yet still deliberately he took aim at the departing car and fired — a single shot.

The Range Rover swerved into the crash barrier, scraped along it for a meter or so amid screams of tortured metal, and stopped.

The man in the high visibility jacket who had signaled to the bus stepped up to the driver's side of the Range Rover and peered into it.

He whistled softly, then looked back at the young man.

"My God," he said, "you've properly done for him."

"I'm afraid I have," the young man said. "I'm sorry. He was quite good. He caught me by surprise with that punch and after that there really wasn't time to mess around."

"Well, you've saved the lives of about fifty children, not to mention their teachers, so thank you. A brilliant shot."

The young man nodded.

"I'm glad it was some use."

"Um — your car's a bit of a wreckage. Can we help? Maybe give you a lift somewhere?"

The young man shook his head and smiled.

"That's all right. There's a friend of mine back there in the queue. She'll take me where I need to go. Goodbye."

He walked away slowly, back down the line of waiting traffic.

After he'd gone about a hundred meters a car door opened and he got in.

The man who'd signaled to the bus didn't see which car it was.

"Who on earth pulled *that* off?" Cecilia said when she heard the story.

"As to that, DCI Cavaliere, neither you nor I will ever know," the chief superintendent said. "I dare say he'll have to testify in court, but it'll be anonymously, from behind closed curtains, with an affidavit from his commanding officer. I'll just give you one clue—if Father Michael has time for an extra prayer tonight, you might ask him please to say one for me, thanking God for United Kingdom Special Forces and the S.A.S.!"

FORTY-EIGHT

Exeter Cathedral Close. Later that morning.

It was Cecilia who spotted Louis Cartwright.

"Over there," she said, "By the county war memorial. In the brown overcoat and hat with his coat collar turned up. I knew it. He couldn't resist coming to see the show!"

Then—

"My God, look at him!" Verity said. "The creep actually means to film it!"

The big blue and yellow tour bus was pulling slowly into the Close, and as it slowed Cartwright raised a camera, steadied himself against the railings, and began to film.

Cecilia nodded to the uniformed constables.

They moved quickly but discreetly through the crowds, careful to avoid Cartwright's line of sight, which wasn't difficult to do since he never took his eyes off the bus.

The constables closed in on either side of him just as Cecilia and Verity stepped in front of his camera.

"Hello, Mr. Cartwright," Cecilia said. "Come to see the results of your handiwork, have you? There's no need to skulk here by the war memorial, you know. You're quite safe. We removed your bomb some time ago."

Cartwright blanched.

"You two!" he said faintly.

"Yes," she said. "Us two! We've been taking bets on whether you'd be idiot enough to come here. I won. For now, I'm going to charge you with conniving at the unlawful assault and detention of two police officers. A relative triviality, but it'll do for the moment. Later on of course we'll have other rather more serious matters to discuss."

Louis Cartwright stood numb and dumb as Cecilia formally arrested and cautioned him. He scarcely reacted even when one of the constables took away his camera and the other placed him in handcuffs.

Passersby stared curiously at the tall gentleman in a well-cut overcoat and handcuffs as he was escorted through their midst, had his hat removed, and was then inserted (with care lest he bump his balding head) into a waiting police car.

As soon as the car drove off, Cecilia looked back to the cathedral. The children in their school uniforms were now off the bus, and teachers were organizing them into parties. Excited voices and laughter came to her across the green. Behind the children the façade of the cathedral glowed warm and welcoming. The blue and yellow tour bus was backing away cautiously.

A boy and girl in school uniforms were walking slowly towards her, evidently wrapped up in each other, hand in hand. The other children from the bus seemed all to be going into the cathedral with the teachers, but these two clearly felt they had something more interesting to do. Their first taste of young love? They stopped for a moment and the girl leaned against the boy. He said something to her and she laughed and kissed his cheek. Then they walked on slowly. Puppy love, of course—surely neither of them could be more than twelve? But not therefore to be scorned! In years to come perhaps one or both of them would look back to this day as the day when they first experienced the enchantment that only the presence of a beloved other can create.

And it could all so easily have been different.

"*All this,*" Susanna had said, "*it's precious. But it's vulnera-ble.... Try to take care of it for us, will you?*"

And if it weren't for Joseph and his pals deciphering those encryptions...

And even then, if they'd taken just an hour or so longer to do it...

Cecilia drew in her breath sharply.

Best not go there.

FORTY-NINE

The same, a few minutes later.

"So have we caught the mighty Teflon?" Verity asked.

Cecilia looked back at her and considered.

"I don't know," she said at last, frowning. "Perhaps we'll know after they've questioned him. Somehow, it all seemed a bit too easy. Cartwright *is* clever, as it turns out, and he's up to his eyes in all this. Yet... well, somehow I expected Teflon to have rather more weight, more *caliber*—"

There was a call on her mobile.

"DI Cav—DCI Cavaliere here."

It was Chief Superintendent Davies.

"Look, Cavaliere, I've received some rather odd information, and I'd like your take on it."

"Sir?"

"Our friend Joseph and his FBI and Europol friends have been trawling. Basically, looking on the Internet for information on everyone who's been connected with U.N.I.T.E.D. in any way. Including, more or less for form's sake, Sir James Harlow."

Almost automatically, at the mention of Sir James's name Cecilia glanced up at Harlow House, which was down from them along the cathedral yard on the right, past the Edinburgh

Woollen Mill. She immediately looked away again, but in the instant that her eyes were trained on the house she could swear she saw a curtain twitch in an upper room, as if someone had stepped away from the window in a hurry.

"Most of what they came across," Davies was saying, "is all about what a great man he is, achievements, honorary degrees, the stuff you'd expect. But then, almost by accident, the computer did present them with one very odd fact. You know the robberies that Teflon pulled off in Stockholm and New York? Well, at the time they took place, Sir James Harlow was in those cities. Nothing to connect him with the crimes, of course—he'd been sent there both times by HM government to act for them. But it's a bit of a coincidence."

"And what about Milan?"

"Well, I gather they simply can't find *where* he was then. But still, when you think of all the places he might have been, two out of three's quite long odds, isn't it? And *maybe* a third, since we just don't know."

"It *is* long odds."

Indeed it was more than long odds. It was a thing odd in itself.

And she'd just seen a curtain twitch in Harlow House.

Did that mean that Sir James was here now in Exeter? Which would make *three* out of *four*—against which the odds were even longer?

At which thought a number of other things came together in her mind.

When she and Verity were prisoners in the U.N.I.T.E.D. tower, she'd thought how tricky it must be keeping Sir James from knowing about the experiments on illegal immigrants.

But then, she'd simply assumed the great man was honest.

Which meant she'd ignored that cardinal principle of detection: *What we can't show we don't know.*

But now, suddenly, unexpected and unwanted, the possibility of a wholly different narrative presented itself to her.

What if Sir James were *not* honest? What if the great man *did* know about the experiments on illegal immigrants? What if his old friend Cartwright—*they were friends together at Oxford,* the chief superintendent had said—what if his old friend had kept him informed all the time? What if *Grieg* was the one being deceived—and then, when things got hot, dumped?

And what if Michael's instincts about Sir James from the beginning had been right? *I find him disturbing. There seem to be two men there, and I don't know who the other one is.*

"So," the chief superintendent was saying, "while it's very embarrassing for us to be questioning someone who's virtually a national hero, I think we need at least to talk to him. He's supposed to be coming in to U.N.I.T.E.D. this afternoon, but I'd really like us to get to him before then if we can."

Cecilia sighed.

"Sir, I think I know where he is. Actually, I think he may be here in Exeter. Should I check it out?"

"Do that," he said. "Use your initiative, and let me know what happens."

Cecilia slipped her phone into her shoulder bag and turned to Verity. Briefly, she explained the situation and her new thoughts about Sir James Harlow.

"Let's walk this way," she said, and led them slowly towards Harlow House. When they arrived at the front door, she tried the brass doorknob. To her surprise, the door opened.

"Leaving the door unlocked somehow doesn't seem like something a guilty man would do," she said.

It was important to be fair.

But Verity said, "What if he's a guilty man who's expecting Cartwright to join him after the bomb goes off, and Cartwright doesn't have a key?"

Cecilia nodded.

"That's possible," she said.

It was indeed possible. Sir James himself had said that Harlow House was his own private little spot.

"DS Jones," she said, "call for some backup on your mobile, and keep your eye on the door, will you? If I'm not out in five minutes come in and get me."

"Yes, ma'am."

Cecilia opened the door and entered.

FIFTY

Harlow House in the Exeter Cathedral Close.
A few minutes later.

Harlow House, as beautiful inside as out, was furnished in exquisite taste. Cecilia suspected it looked much as it had in the days of the beautiful mistress who liked to go to church.

"Hello!" she called out. "Is anyone at home?"

No answer.

She peered into rooms on each side of the hall. In one of them, over the chimney piece, was a painting of a young woman in Victorian dress. The beautiful mistress?

She mounted the stairs, which were well built and heavily carpeted. She came to a landing. Across the way from her was an open door, and through it she could see Sir James Harlow. He was by one of the windows, peering through a gap between drawn curtains of heavy brocade.

She walked quietly to the doorway and stood for a moment, watching him. Apparently he was too preoccupied to notice her — too preoccupied even to have registered her call when she entered the house.

She would try a long shot.

"Are you still waiting for the bus to explode?" she said.

He swung round.

Until that moment, despite what the chief superintendent had told her, despite Verity's guess, despite her own questions and Michael's instincts—despite all, she'd entertained a tiny shred of hope that the timing of those visits to Stockholm and New York was an unfortunate coincidence.

The look on Sir James's face as he turned put an end to that. She saw what Michael had sensed from the beginning—saw the man beneath the mask that had just slipped, and wondered how on earth she could have missed seeing some hint of it.

She took a deep breath and let loose more long shots.

"The bus won't explode," she said, walking into the room. "We've removed the bomb. Vasily's dead. Your friend Cartwright's under arrest. So there's only you left."

Silence. It didn't last long.

"Look," he said, "Cecilia—I may call you Cecilia, mayn't I?" She shrugged.

"Cecilia, I know this looks awful."

Dear God, he was starting to negotiate. He was assuming she knew what she had merely guessed. And now, of course, she did know. In effect he'd just told her.

"Honestly, though, it isn't as bad as it seems," he said.

"You and your friends just tried to blow up a bus full of school children," she said. "So explain to me how that isn't as bad as it seems."

He looked away from her and put his hand to his forehead.

"Oh my God, I'm so glad that didn't come off—that those kids are all right. Blowing up a tour bus was Louis Cartwright's plan. He came up with it some weeks ago. I think he'd been influenced by Vasily, who as far as I'm concerned is just a thug we employ occasionally—a thug who oughtn't to have any influence at all. Anyway, when Cartwright broached the idea I told him I was appalled. So he said he'd put it on hold. I thought that meant it was postponed indefinitely or even abandoned. But then yesterday, mid-afternoon, he phones and says a golden opportunity has come up. Unexpected circumstances have enabled him to create a situation whereby on Thursday night the attention of Exeter CID is almost certain to be focused on U.N.I.T.E.D. There's a school bus the following morning that'll be a perfect target for an explosion. And Vasily has operational groups in Exeter ready to take out three banks. So Cartwright's told them to get on with it. When I lit into him for doing this without consulting me, he said there hadn't been time to consult, the chance was too good to miss, and now he'd given them the go ahead there wasn't anything he could do to stop it anyway. Vasily and the groups would all be incommunicado until the operation was complete. I was stunned. Horrified. But what could I do?"

Cecilia raised an eyebrow.

"It will be interesting to see if Cartwright corroborates your version of events," she said.

"Frankly Cecilia, I've no idea what Louis Cartwright will say. I've known him for years and I thought he was my friend. Now I'm no longer sure I know him at all. But you must believe me. What I've told you is the truth. I swear it."

"Well," she said, "even if it is, that hardly makes your part in what's happened all right, does it? If you were really horrified, why didn't you do your duty as a citizen and inform us? An anonymous tipoff would have been something. It wasn't rocket science. And what about your other colleague, the charming Herbert Grieg?"

"Grieg is a computer genius—"

"He's also a homicidal criminal."

Sir James sighed—a long sigh, a deeply felt sigh.

"Alas, that's true. And I'd realized it. I thought at first that his work might produce some real benefits for the human race, but he'd turned into a loose cannon. Honestly, Cecilia, Cartwright and I had already decided to let him go."

"Leaving him to face the music. Actually, we'd more or less worked that out. Well, leaving aside your complicity in Grieg's crimes—and it's hardly a triviality—what about the blood diamonds? What about the deaths in New York and Stockholm and Milan?"

Another sigh, this one less dramatic.

"Cecilia, let's face facts."

Why is it that I never trust people who tell me to face facts?

"If I hadn't provided arms to those people in Africa," Sir James said, "someone else would have, and if no one else did they'd kill each other with machetes. As for New York, the Hogan warehouse was empty except for Hogan. It was a sweatshop and everyone knew it. Hogan was a sod who took advantage of illegals and worked them into the ground."

"That didn't give *you* the right to kill him."

"I did the world a favor by eliminating him. In Stockholm no one was hurt at all, those exploding cars just made a good firework display. As for Milan?" He frowned and shook his head. "I am truly sorry about that." She had to admit it—he actually looked as if he was. "Those three kids were killed and the others injured only because the damned school had changed its schedule and we didn't know. The playground should have been empty."

"It was still your explosives that killed and maimed them," Cecilia said. "I dare say one day you may find yourself explaining how that wasn't your fault to the Italian police. In the meantime, I'm not arresting you for any of those crimes but because you've been complicit in placing an explosive device on a bus full of children and their teachers on a school trip, a reckless endangerment of life to which you've just admitted. And to which, incidentally—in case you decide to change your story—I have your admission recorded. As I also have you admitting to the crimes that were committed in New York, Stockholm, and Milan."

She indicated her shoulder bag.

He frowned and shook his head.

"A recording? Surely, Cecilia, you know you won't be able to use that as evidence."

She gave a half smile.

"Probably not. Though I wouldn't count on it. There is such a thing as judge's discretion. And what's admissible as evidence in a criminal trial is actually a matter of some debate just at present. It's all these technological developments, you know!"

She paused. She could feel her mouth tightening.

"But what matters," she continued, " — the fact, Sir James, that you need to face — is that I now know you're guilty. And I intend to make sure my colleagues know it, too. And then we can start building a case against you. And just think of all the resources we've got — not just the CID but the FBI, Europol, Interpol, the lot. Sooner or later we will find the evidence to convict you. You can be sure of that."

FIFTY-ONE

The same, a few minutes later.

Sir James stood for a moment looking at Cecilia. Or *was* he looking at her? Was he really seeing her at all? He seemed distant, preoccupied, as if he were trying to decide what to say next.

Finally, it came.

"Cecilia, while all this is still just between us, may I ask you to think about one more thing before you play that recording to anyone or arrest me? Would you be willing at least to listen to what I've been doing for the last two weeks and what its result is likely to be?"

Interested despite herself, she nodded.

"All right. This is it. Everyone knows that over the last month or so the Syrian government's been charged with using chemical weapons against its own people, the Russians have said if chemical weapons were used it was probably by the rebels, and the American president's boxed himself into a corner by saying chemical weapons are a red line that can't be crossed, meaning the U.S. will take military action. Fortunately, at least he's been smart enough to ask Congress for their backing before he starts a war, which has given us a bit of time. That's what's known of the story so far."

"*I* certainly know it, Sir James. Could you get to the part that should make me think twice about arresting you?"

"Just listen to the part of the story everyone *doesn't* know. I've spent the last two weeks as Her Majesty's special envoy, charging back and forth between the UN, the White House, and the Russians, first persuading them it was worth listening to me at all—no easy matter, since Britain's no longer a great power—and then getting them to listen to each other."

He paused, seeming to sort the facts in his mind.

"So, as a result of all that charging about, here's what I believe will happen over the next week or so. A UN report will say that chemical weapons *have* been used in the Syrian conflict but won't say who used them or attribute blame. Russia will then surprise everybody by suggesting the Syrian government should place its chemical weapons under international control so they can be destroyed, and the Syrians will have to agree, since Russia's their major supporter. The Americans will have gained a face-saving way to get out of a war, and the Russians will have gained lots of brownie points as global peacemakers. Even the Syrians will be able to claim victory of a sort, since they'll have avoided being attacked by the Americans. And most important, thousands of lives—indeed, more likely *hundreds* of thousands—will have been saved."

How on earth could a man who was involved in this sort of work also be a man who would be complicit—as complicit he was, however much he might protest—in blowing up a bus full of school children? Michael had been right. It was as if one were dealing with two entirely different people.

"These," Sir James said, "are things I can—well, perhaps not bring about, Cecilia, but at least help others to bring about. It's something I seem to have a gift for, perhaps a unique gift. Do you really want to bring that work to an end? Because that's what you're going to do if you arrest me. If you disgrace me. I've caused some deaths, and I would give a great deal not to have done so. I profoundly regret every one of them. But I have *saved* the lives of thousands.

"And I can save more. That ill-judged war we insisted on fighting in Iraq has left the entire area unstable. The Sunni-Shia divide could blow up there at any time and God knows what that will lead to: there are Sunni elements that could seek to establish a caliphate. Doubtless the Israelis and the Palestinians will continue their madness. And lately I'm worried about Russia — hardly anyone in the west, it seems to me, sees yet the extent of Putin's ambition, or of his fears. He has his eyes on Ukraine. Which means, Cecilia, that believe me, the world will go on needing skills like mine for a long time."

While he was speaking, Verity had come quietly into the room with two uniformed constables. Cecilia nodded to them, and turned back to Sir James.

"I do believe you," she said. "And it's nothing to the point."

It wasn't until this moment that she realized how angry she was. His charm, his good manners, his kindness, his political insights, his negotiating brilliance, his ability to sum up the world situation — they were all part of him, but he used them. They were a trick, a seduction, and she had let herself be seduced.

"Sir James," she said, "you've been a hero to me ever since you took the trouble to come over and speak to me that day at Lancaster House when I was just a PC. And now I feel I've been a complete fool. You do have an astonishing gift that's benefitted the world again and again. You have skills that the world desperately needs. I can see that. But unfortunately you're also a ruthless crook."

He flinched.

"I *don't* like putting a stop to your work, Sir James. Perhaps you really do regret the things you've done. But I'm just a police officer and I don't get to pick and choose which laws I'll enforce. And in any case, when it comes to breaking the law, I'm afraid *profoundly regretting* doesn't count. After all, it's not exactly as if you were asking me to overlook a traffic violation, is it?"

She took a deep breath.

"Sir James Harlow, I am arresting you…"

In terms that were as measured as she could manage, given her feelings, she recited the form of arrest and the caution.

He stood before her, silent, head down until she finished.

"You do not have to say anything but it may harm your defense if you do not mention when questioned something which you later rely on in court. Anything you do say may be given in evidence. Do you understand this?"

He straightened up and met her eyes.

"Yes," he said. "Alas, I do understand it."

FIFTY-TWO

Exeter Cathedral Close, about ten minutes later.

Exercising the discretion allowed to arresting police officers in Britain, Cecilia had chosen not to place Sir James in handcuffs. Even so, as he was escorted between two constables to a waiting police car and inserted into it, it was rather evident that he was in custody. More than one passerby recognized the well-known figure, and there were some expressions of surprise.

Cecilia telephoned Chief Superintendent Davies and told him what had happened.

Davies sighed heavily.

"My God, is this going to cause a flap!"

"I expect it will, sir."

"Anyway, it's done. And overall this is a very good result. Good work by everyone."

"Thank you, sir. And now, if it's all the same to you, DS Jones and I need to go and get something to eat. I seem to have been running on tea and adrenalin since I can't remember when."

"Of course, Cavaliere! I should have thought of that myself. We can handle things here. Come in when you've eaten. You and DS Jones take your time. We'll deal with Harlow."

Cecilia shook her head as she put the phone back into her bag.

The great man had been "Sir James" to them all. But since ten minutes ago he was a man under arrest—a man for the police to "deal with."

From now on he was just "Harlow."

"Strictly speaking, ma'am," Verity said as they walked along, "since you implied to Sir James that you might have overlooked a traffic violation, it seems to me you conceded in principle that you *do* pick and choose which laws to enforce."

Cecilia smiled.

"I'm afraid I'm not consistent."

"Actually, even though you're not always completely logical it seems to me you generally make the right decision."

"Well, thank you, Verity... I think."

"Don't mention it! And when he tried on all that stuff about how you'd be stopping his good works you certainly put him down—good and proper, as Sergeant Wyatt would say!"

Cecilia laughed. Verity could manage a passable Scottish brogue, but her attempts at Devonian were atrocious.

"Verity," she said, "I must admit I've found the whole business incredibly depressing."

"It's hard to find one's hero isn't a hero," Verity said.

"Well, yes, it is. But that's not what I meant. I meant my complete failure to see there was something wrong with him."

"When you decided all those years ago that he was a good man, maybe he *was* a good man, or at least as good as any of us are."

"But when I saw him this morning, the fact that he'd changed since then screamed at me. It's frustrating that I missed it until now—especially when Michael saw it so clearly."

"We all make mistakes sometimes," Verity said. "I must admit, when we met him outside the U.N.I.T.E.D. tower yesterday, I thought he was lovely!"

They walked on for a few yards in comfortable silence.

Then Verity said, "I've just been reading about one of those psychologists who *specialize* in reading what's going on with people — he trained with Paul Ekman, had a long record of successes, the lot. He was working with the army in Belfast in 1989. One afternoon he interviewed a suspect for two hours, saw nothing violent or dangerous in the man, and on his say-so the army let him go. Three hours later the fellow walked into a pub and shot four people dead. That didn't mean the psychologist wasn't any good. It's just that everyone misses stuff sometimes. Actually, most times you and Michael both seem to me to have an extraordinary instinct for picking up on what's going on with people. Most times. But no one's infallible."

Cecilia nodded.

"I expect my problem is mostly hurt pride."

"Probably," Verity said.

Cecilia smiled to herself. No use expecting Verity Jones to beat about the bush!

"And Sir James is *such* a muddle of good and bad," Verity continued. "No wonder he's hard to read. I doubt he can read himself. I'm sorry for him in a way."

"*'For where an unclean mind carries virtuous qualities, their commendations go with pity; they are virtues and traitors too.'*"

"That's exactly it! You didn't just say that out of your head, did you, ma'am?"

"It's Shakespeare. *All's Well That Ends Well.*"

"Oh. I thought it had guts in it! Not that your words don't, of course."

"That's all right, Verity. I don't mind coming in second to Shakespeare."

They walked on until they came to the Côte Brasserie with its striped awning and chairs and tables waiting optimistically outside.

"I told Chief Superintendent Davies we need to eat," she said. "I do, anyway. They do decent French cooking in there, and good coffee. Shall we go?"

"Yes, let's."

They both ordered *moules marinières* starters to be followed by roast sea bass for Verity and fish *parmentier* for Cecilia.

"Excellent choice, madam," the waiter said to each of them.

"Do you think," Cecilia said when he'd left, "he ever says, 'That's a terrible choice! Pick *anything* on the menu but that?"

"Maybe when he gets back to the kitchen he says, 'I'd be *ashamed* to have ordered this!"

"*Deeply* and *bitterly* ashamed!'"

They both giggled.

"Ma'am," Verity said, suddenly serious, "do you remember what you said to Grieg when we were in the U.N.I.T.E.D. tower—about me being already taken?"

"Yes, Verity."

"Well I'm glad you said that, ma'am. I'm glad you've realized I'm going to marry Joseph."

"That's wonderful, Verity. I didn't realize you two were already engaged."

Verity blushed. "Well, we're not, actually. At least, Joseph doesn't know about it yet."

"Ah! So when is he going to know?"

"I think he'll be ready quite soon. Then I'll tell him. But he's so anxious—about being black, he thinks it'll make life harder for me. And then if we have children, life will be harder for them. And he may well be right. But everyone has their problems."

"You're both so beautiful and intelligent, I imagine it's likely your children will be beautiful and intelligent too."

"That's what I think," Verity said. "And Father Spee said we were making a fitting progress. So I think it will be all right. But Joseph will need some careful handling."

Cecilia smiled. You sound more like my mama every day.

FIFTY-THREE

Edgestow, the U.N.I.T.E.D. tower.
The same night, about 11.30 pm.

"Did you see that mackerel sky earlier?" Sergeant Wyatt said.

He and PC Wilkins had completed their inspection of the tower and were back in the atrium. The building was still cordoned off as a crime scene, and Sergeant Wyatt had volunteered himself to cover the first session looking after the tower with Wilkins. They were to be relieved at midnight.

"I did, Sergeant. *Mares' tails and mackerel scales, tall ships take in their sails.* That's what my grandmother says. And there was that nasty, gusty wind."

"Yes," Wyatt said, "fretful it was, like the trees were in a fever. I think there'll be thunder. I always get a headache before a thunderstorm, and I've had one for — hello, what's that?"

He could hear a dull roar, as from a distance, but where?

"I don't know," Wilkins said. "It sounds almost like a — Jesus Christ!"

Both men staggered. The chandeliers over their heads swayed. A stack of papers on a desk slid to the edge and fell to the floor.

Then it stopped. Silence.

"*That,*" Wyatt said, "was an earth tremor. Mrs. Wyatt and I were in one once in Portsmouth. It was—good God almighty!"

Both men reeled and grabbed at the furniture. The chandeliers swung violently and everything not fastened down went spinning. A couple of colored plastic ducks bounced and ricocheted across the floor. The lights went out. There were sounds of rumbling and splintering above and around them. Dust and rubble tumbled down on their heads.

Then it was over. Another silence. The lights came back on.

They looked at each other.

"That wasn't an earth *tremor,*" Sergeant Wyatt said. "That was an earth*quake.*"

As he brushed a piece of plaster from the sleeve of his uniform, another piece dropped onto it.

"Look at the roof, Sergeant. And the wall."

He looked.

A long crack had appeared in the ceiling, a hairline at one end of the reception area that widened to a fissure five or six centimeters wide at the other. There was another crack in the wall opposite them. And as he stared at it the wall above it shifted to the right and the crack began to lengthen.

If he went and got himself killed in here, Mrs. Wyatt would never forgive him.

Especially after he'd gone and volunteered for the duty.

More rumblings and creaks from the ceiling above them.

"Constable," he said, "tactical withdrawal! On the double!"

"On it, Sergeant!"

The two of them bolted through the big glass doors and were out fifty meters into the car park when they heard another rumble from behind them.

Wyatt turned to look—and again lurched, as the ground swayed beneath him.

The lights in the tower had gone out again. Blocks of rubble fell near it. There was a sustained roar—then what looked like a concrete ledge came crashing down, blocking what had been the main entrance. Lights were coming on in buildings in the surrounding complex. He could hear doors slamming and excited voices.

But the tower was still dark.

A couple of Eglītis security, young men still in their gray uniforms but now without their MP5s, ran up and joined them.

"Are you both well?" one of them said breathlessly in his Latvian accent. "Can we help you?"

"We're well enough," Wyatt said, "but I doubt the tower is. Thank God there's no one inside. I reckon the ground floor ceiling's come down completely. In fact I think the whole inside's collapsed."

The four of them stood surveying the scene.

"Wasn't this tower supposed to be earthquake-proof?" Wilkins said.

Wyatt grimaced.

"Apparently not."

"You realize, Sergeant, if we'd still been upstairs..."

"Yes, Constable," Wyatt said quietly. "I do."

From the west they could now hear police sirens and see the intermittent flash of blue and white lights. From the sky to the east more lights and the clatter of an approaching helicopter. Evidently someone had scrambled the Eurocopter.

"What should we do?" the other Latvian said, a fresh-faced boy who looked shaken and scared, though evidently doing his best to put a brave face on it.

"Nothing at all, lad," Sergeant Wyatt said gently. "You're doing fine. The cavalry is on its way."

It dawned on him that his headache had gone.

Well, that was something, wasn't it? It was an ill wind that blew nobody any good.

Still, it was a hell of an expensive way to cure a headache.

Two police cars, lights flashing and sirens blaring, swung into view and pulled up at the other end of the car park, their lights continuing to flash although the sirens died. Chief

Superintendent Davies himself and several other officers spilled out of them.

"We're over here, sir!" Wyatt shouted. "All present and correct. Nobody's hurt."

The relief on the chief superintendent's face as he and the others ran over to them was evident.

"You're sure there was no one else in there, Sergeant?" Davies said.

More sirens and lights to the west confirmed that emergency services were on their way.

"Yes, sir. Constable Wilkins and I had just done a patrol of the place, all twenty floors and the extra one, right before it happened. Took us over an hour. It was definitely empty."

"Thank God for that," Davies said.

The group stood for several minutes surveying the scene. The Eurocopter was now directly overhead. The roar of its engines and the relentless clatter of its blades were deafening. Its searchlight beamed down directly onto the tower, revealing clouds of dust and broken stone. From behind them the flashing lights of police cars were reflected in a slab of the darkened tower's glass.

Sergeant Wyatt shook his head and turned to Wilkins.

"Well, my lad," —he shouted to make himself heard—"it looks as if you and me are in for it good and proper when the chief constable hears about this."

"Why's that, Sergeant?"

"That was a perfectly good tower, that was. All shiny bright and almost brand new. And what happens? They leave you and me to keep an eye on it for a couple of hours, and now look at the mess it's in!"

FIFTY-FOUR

Saint Mary's Rectory, Exeter. The following morning.
About 9.00 a.m.

The next day was a Saturday. Since coming to Exeter Michael had chosen, whenever possible, to take Saturday as his day off. This tended to fit Cecilia's schedule (insofar as she had one) better than the Wednesdays he'd taken when he was in London. And, as he could not resist pointing out from time to time to anyone who would listen, despite what some Christians claimed about Sunday, the scriptures made it clear that it was actually Saturday, the seventh day, that was the true Sabbath—God's appointed day of rest, the day Christ rested in the tomb. Certainly Sunday had its own and greater glories, being the day of new creation, the day of the Lord's resurrection. But those things, wonderful though they were, did not make Sunday the Sabbath.

There was no early celebration, so he and Cecilia slept quite late.

They were more or less stirring, however, when Papa knocked at their bedroom door and entered, accompanied by Figaro, at their invitation. He brought them coffee and brioches, along with the news that Rachel had finished her breakfast and was now supervising Mama as she gave various creatures theirs, after which the whole lot of them would then go out for a walk. So there was no need for Michael and Cecilia to worry about anything.

"And by the way, your institute's in the news again," he added as he was starting to leave.

"What is it this time?" Cecilia asked.

"Quite a serious earthquake in Edgestow, just before midnight last night. Three point nine on the Richter scale. No one was hurt, but it brought much of the U.N.I.T.E.D. tower down. It said on the news that the tremor was felt in Exeter, though I must admit it didn't wake me up, or Rosina. I don't even think the dogs barked."

"That doesn't surprise me," Michael said. "Unless they think there's some immediate danger to us, I've noticed our dogs tend to be a pretty dozy bunch. Quite uninterested in what's happening fifty or so miles away."

Cecilia giggled.

"The cats," Michael added, "would of course be completely useless even if we were being broken into by armed hooligans."

"True," Papa said. "But I'll tell you who *is* getting excited — the politicians and the scientists! There's already been a statement from the Home Secretary saying the British Geological Survey's report must have been in error, and another from BGS saying on the contrary, when the U.N.I.T.E.D. tower was being built key qualifications in the BGS report were ignored. A nice row brewing, I think. Enjoy your coffee! I'm going to finish my breakfast and enjoy the walk."

He left, closing the door behind him as soon as Figaro, having wagged "good morning" to Cecilia on her side of the bed and Michael on his, had followed him through it — still wagging, and doubtless drawn by the mention of breakfast.

Michael lay and watched as his wife sat up and ate her brioche and drank her *caffè*. The truth was, even after nearly four years of marriage, he was still somewhat in awe of the fact that Cecilia allowed him to share her bed. And her disappearance the day before had made him only the more conscious of that privilege. So he now gazed up at her with a pleasure he made no attempt to disguise while she ate and drank.

She looked down at him, then raised an eyebrow.

"Good morning, Italian lady policeman," he said.

"Good morning, vicar that's married to her," she replied, and returned to her brioche.

She finished it, wiped her fingers on one of the napkins Papa had obligingly left on the tray, and poured for herself a second *caffè*. It wasn't until she was about to drink it that Michael realized she was asking him a question.

"So what do you think?" she said.

"I'm sorry. I didn't hear what you said. Think about what?"

She smiled, surely not unaware that she herself had been the cause of his distraction.

"So what do you think about the U.N.I.T.E.D. tower falling down?"

"I think I'm jolly glad you weren't still in it."

"So am I. And apart from that?"

"Well, after all you told me about the goings on there, I suppose I could be tempted to say, 'God is not mocked.'"

"And will you?"

"I don't think so. I think I'll just say 'bad planning,' and leave God to decide what God had to do with it."

"I see."

She finished her *caffè* and slid down beside him, her face towards his on the pillow.

"And what do you think about Grieg's plan to download himself into silicon and live forever?"

He considered.

"It sounds boring," he said finally.

"That's what I thought."

There was a sudden clattering at the door.

"*Mamma, mamma, posso entrare?* Daddy, Daddy, may I come in?"

This entreaty was accompanied by a couple of woofs that seemed to mean much the same thing.

They both sat up, Cecilia rearranging the bedclothes, then spoke at the same time.

"*Sì, tesoro! Puoi entrare!*"

"Yes, sweetheart! Come in!"

Figaro and Rachel more or less fell into the room together. Figaro bounded this way and that around the bed while there tumbled from Rachel an excited rush of English and Italian.

"Daddy, you know what Figaro and I found in the garden?! *Mamma, sapete che abbiamo trovato nel giardino?!*"

Michael exchanged a glance with Cecilia.

"No sweetheart," he said, "we don't know. But I think it's quite likely you're going to tell us!"

EPILOGUE

Saint Mary's Rectory, Exeter. After lunch on the same day.

Cecilia, who'd been given the rest of the weekend off, had taken Rachel upstairs to the bedroom for a nap.

Figaro, Tocco, and Pu had followed them.

Michael was in front of his computer at the desk in his study.

Felix and Marlene were in a pile on what seemed somehow over the last couple of weeks to have become *their* armchair.

Michael pursed his lips and made a small change in the text of tomorrow's sermon.

The telephone rang.

He waited. It was, after all, supposed to be his day off.

"Hello," a voice said after the answerphone had given its usual message about this being Saint Mary's Rectory, "This is the administrator of Exeter Prison, and I'm calling on behalf of the governor. We'd like to have a word with Father Michael Aarons if that's possible."

"Oh Lord," he muttered.

He reached across and picked up the handset.

"Hello," he said, "this is Michael Aarons."

"Good afternoon, Father. We have a prisoner remanded in custody here awaiting trial, Sir James Harlow. We believe you know him. Owing to the seriousness of the charges, bail's been refused."

"Yes," Michael said. "I do know him, slightly."

"Well, Father, he wants to make his confession. We do have a full time Anglican chaplain, but Harlow says he particularly wants you to be his confessor. The governor says she's willing to allow it if you're willing to come and do it."

Michael sighed.

He looked out of the window — it was starting to rain.

"I can be there in about twenty-five minutes," he said.

H.M. Prison Exeter, at 30 New North Road, was a red brick Victorian building. Michael found the mere look of it intimidating. The thought of being incarcerated there appalled him.

But then, the thought of being incarcerated anywhere appalled him.

He parked his car and got out. It was by now raining heavily. He turned up his raincoat collar, wished he'd had sense enough to bring an umbrella, and walked towards the entrance — quickly, because he was not enjoying getting wet, yet reluctantly, too, because he didn't really want to go inside the place.

As he mounted the steps, the dark, heavy door opened and a woman came out to meet him.

"Good afternoon, Father," she said. "I'm the governor. Come inside — you must be soaked."

Michael complied, glad to get out of what had become a downpour. He removed his raincoat, which was, fortunately, a good one.

"Thank you for coming so quickly," she said. "And without any notice at all."

"Some things are important," he said. "I was thinking — hoping — perhaps this might be one of them, at least for James Harlow."

The governor nodded.

"They've set up a prie-dieu for the penitent," she said as they walked to the chapel, "and a seat beside it for you in the sanctuary. That's what our chaplain uses. Technically we're not supposed to leave you alone with the prisoner, but the officer will wait for him outside the chapel door at the far end, where he can see both of you through the window but can't hear you. Does that sound all right?"

"It sounds just right," Michael said with a smile.

Michael finished a brief prayer for grace for himself and the penitent, then stood and waited. He was glad to see there was a crucifix in front of the prie-dieu, placed so that the penitent could see it.

There was the sound of a key being turned, then a subdued clatter at the end of the nave.

He looked up.

The door at the back of the chapel had a glass window through which he could see the head and peaked cap of a prison officer. The door opened and Sir James entered, alone.

"Father Michael," he said, "this is very good of you."

Michael smiled and shook his head.

"Have you made your confession before, Sir James?" he asked quietly.

"There was a time when I was a regular penitent. I know what to do, if that's what you mean."

"It is. Good. Then we may begin whenever you are ready."

Michael indicated the prie-dieu, seated himself beside it, adjusted his stole, made sure there were tissues handy, and prepared to listen.

Sir James sank to his knees.

"Bless me, Father, for I have sinned."

"The Lord be in your heart and on your lips that you may truly and humbly confess your sins."

"I confess to almighty God, before the whole company of heaven and before you…"

Michael leaned towards him, cupping his chin in his hand

as he always did when hearing confessions, doing his best to concentrate with grace.

Sir James's confession was, as Michael had expected of him, intelligent, well prepared, and full. He spared (so far as Michael could tell) neither detail nor himself.

"In 2002 I committed a terrible breach of trust. I was brought in to help with a situation that looked similar to the Omani affair—a young couple arrested for carrying drugs, only this time in Saudi Arabia. But in fact the situations weren't similar at all. This time it wasn't a pair of young fools bringing a bit of pot into the country for their own amusement. This was a pair of young but experienced criminals trafficking hard drugs for massive profit. The Saudi authorities had evidence, *and I knew it*. I knew it because only hours after their arrest members of the young man's family came to me in panic. They told me the truth, then offered me a great deal of money if I would help get their son released. Of course, given my position, I should have refused even to see them, let alone listen to their proposal."

He paused.

Michael waited.

"A consultant's fee," Sir James finally said. "That was what I called it. I used my skills—my God-given skills—to get a pair of drug dealers off the hook. And I did it for the money." He sighed and looked down.

Sir James's story continued through contacts made over the next few years in Sierra Leone, the Ivory Coast, and Angola— contacts leading him to the arms trade and blood diamonds, to an ever more expensive lifestyle and an ever increasing need for money.

"I valued the reputation of being a good man," he said, "and in many matters I was one. But I also wanted what they call the good life—and always more than I actually had. I told myself I *needed* to be inordinately wealthy in order to command the necessary respect for my work! Unless I was rich, the people I dealt with wouldn't pay proper attention to all my wisdom. And so I was the servant of two masters."

Abruptly, he stopped.

Michael waited while the penitent seemed to struggle with he had to say next.

"In the end," he said at last, "I let myself be persuaded it didn't matter. I told myself the good I was doing in the world outweighed the evil. After all, I was helping whole nations, wasn't I? Of course I *knew* better. But the fact was, I *wanted* to believe that because I did some good the bad things I did didn't matter much—even when people died as a consequence of them. Collateral damage. It was, after all, such a very *convenient* doctrine."

At which point he started to weep.

Michael passed him a tissue.

"I'm sorry to be blubbing like this," Sir James said when he could speak again. "Forgive me."

"We all have things for which we need to be forgiven," Michael said quietly. "Our tears of contrition are not, I think, among them. Take all the time you need."

At last the story was finished.

"O God, for these and all those sins I cannot now remember, I ask your forgiveness."

A brief pause.

"And of you, Father, I ask penance, advice, and absolution."

Michael took a deep breath.

"You've done well," he said gently. "This can't have been easy. Now for what comes next. First, as a part of your penance, and if you haven't already done so, you must give the authorities a full account of your crimes, especially your crimes against other persons. Your lawyers may advise you to be evasive. I cannot. There can't be the kind of reconciliation that you seek without truth. Once you have told the truth, of course you will still have your rights as a citizen, and you may follow the advice of your lawyers. But you must first be open. If you aren't, the absolution you receive today will be for nothing. It would be better not to have received it. Is that clear?"

"Yes, Father."

"Good. Next, you must try to make some amends. As you pray and think about this, you may think of several areas where this should happen, but I am quite clear about one. You need to do whatever you can to help and support those children and their families who were injured by the explosion in Milan. Perhaps you can set up a fund for them."

"I will, Father. Would you be willing to talk to my accountants and lawyers about how best to do it?"

"I can do that. Before I do, you'll need to tell them what you want me to talk with them about, and you'll need to instruct them to get in touch with me. Otherwise I'll be bound by the secrecy of the confessional and won't be able to say anything."

"Thank you, Father. I'll do that."

"We need also to think about your own spiritual journey from now on. I'd suggest that more than anything you try to practice contentment. I know this may seem hard—but if you can, try to be content with the situation in which you find yourself and with what you have, especially the material things, even in prison."

"With respect, Father, I think prison may be exactly the place for me to learn this. And these last few days—well, we go out and walk around the prison yard in the mornings, and I find I'm looking at the sky and thinking how beautiful it is. There was a bird singing this morning—and I still have ears to hear it!"

Michael nodded.

"It sounds as if you're already beginning to see how rich the life you have really is—even here."

Sir James gave a faint smile.

"Some of the time," he said, "yes."

Again Michael nodded.

There was a moment of silence, then Michael said, "Is there anything else you want to ask me?"

"I don't think so."

"Do you understand that despite all that has happened and whatever may happen in the future, still as a baptized person you are God's child? Christ died for you, and you are an heir to the kingdom of heaven. Nothing and no one in life or death can take that from you, unless you choose to renounce it."

"Yes, Father, I understand that."

"Good. Never forget it. Let it be for a sign upon your hand and frontlets between your eyes."

And now Michael got to his feet and looked down at him.

"Our Lord Jesus Christ," he said, "who has left power to his church to absolve all sinners who truly repent and believe in him, of his great mercy forgive you your offences. And by his authority committed to me"—he extended his hand over the kneeling figure, making the sign of the cross as he spoke—"I absolve you from all your sins, in the name of the Father, and of the Son, and of the Holy Spirit."

"Amen."

"For part of your penance say the General Thanksgiving from the *Book of Common Prayer*."

"Yes, Father."

"Go in peace, and pray for me, a sinner."

AUTHOR'S NOTE

If any imagine that notions of "singularity" entertained by some of the villains in this story are the fruit of my creative imagination, they give me too much credit. Let them try entering "singularity" into the browsers on their computers, and they will learn otherwise. Or else let them read the convenient summary in Lev Grossman's article, "2045: The Year Man Becomes Immortal" (*Time Magazine*, 21th February 2011, 43-49). Of course I don't suggest that all or even any of those who entertain such ideas are villains like Herbert Grieg. But that said, I suspect that is largely because of their own inherent decency, for I cannot deny that — in contrast to more traditional approaches to life, such as the traditional philosophies and religions of which I am aware — the ideas and beliefs generally associated with "singularity" appear to me to offer precious little in the way of compelling reason why one should *not* be a villain like Herbert Grieg.

As will be obvious to those familiar with C. S. Lewis's science fiction, I owe the city of Edgestow to his novel *That Hideous Strength*. Despite Lewis's explicit denial, many scholars think that he intended the University of Edgestow to be the University of Durham. Among these is my friend Robert MacSwain, who knows more about Lewis than I ever will, and with whom I would not dream of arguing. Nevertheless, and despite this weight of opinion, for my own little fiction I have chosen to take Lewis at his word, and so Edgestow is not

Durham or anywhere near it. Since (so far as I can see) Lewis gives no indication where Edgestow is, nor the nearby village of Saint Anne's-on-the-Hill, save of course that they are obviously in England, I have felt free to supply that gap. I understand Edgestow and the village of St. Anne's to be in North Devon, about ninety minutes (more or less) away from Exeter, and not far from the village of Petrockstowe (or Petrockstow). I imagine that the River Wynd eventually flows into the Exe, although I have made no attempt to check this and I may be wrong. To reach Edgestow from Exeter, you would need to go west on the A30 as far as Okehampton, as Cecilia did, and then turn north, although after that promising start I must admit to being somewhat vague. In the 1940s, of course, you could have travelled there on the Great Western Railway.

The Cavalieres' family traditions about the defense of Rome are soundly based. Some historians dismiss the Italians' defense of Rome against the Germans in 1943 as a matter of a few troops who "fought back and were massacred" (Norman Davies, *Europe at War 1939-1945: No Simple Victory* [London: Macmillan, 2006], 181). The reality was not so simple. Even their adversaries admitted that the Italian troops defending Rome in 1943 fought magnificently. Rome fell to the Nazis not because its defenders were defeated by the enemy but because they were betrayed by their commanders. Any who are interested in details of the battle should read Flavio Carbone, "La partecipazione dei Carabinieri alla Difesa di Roma — 8-10 Settembre 1943," on line at http://www.carabinieri.it/Internet/Editoria/Rassegna+Arma/2002/4/Studi/05_Carbone.htm.

Acknowledgements

Last, but certainly not least, I want to say that if there is any virtue or anything to praise in my little fictions, then I am certainly much indebted for that to my many friends who kindly read what I have written and tell me what is wrong with it. To name but the most obvious among my conversation partners, I must surely thank Wendy Bryan, Suzanne Dunstan, John Gatta, Julia Gatta, Bob Hughes, David Landon, Leslie Richardson, Luann Landon, Rob MacSwain, Laurie Ramsey, Barbara Stafford, and Bill Stafford. There is also the matter of editing. Someone asked me the other day how I would recommend anyone to proceed who wished to write fiction. I answered without hesitation, "Find an editor whose judgment you trust, and then *pay attention to what they say!*" Personally, I am immeasurably indebted to Renni Browne, Shannon Roberts, and everyone at The Editorial Department for their help with my efforts over the years, and I cannot thank them too much or recommend them too highly.

Christopher Bryan,
The School of Theology,
Sewanee.
Saint Augustine of Canterbury, 2013.

ABOUT THE AUTHOR

Christopher Bryan is a priest, novelist, and academic living and working in Sewanee, Tennessee and Exeter, England. His earlier novels are *Siding Star* (Diamond Press, 2012) and *Peacekeeper* (Diamond Press, 2013). His academic studies include *Listening to the Bible* (Oxford University Press, 2014), *The Resurrection of the Messiah* (Oxford University Press, 2011), and *Render to Caesar: Jesus, the Early Church, and the Roman Superpower* (Oxford University Press, 2005).

CPSIA information can be obtained at www.ICGtesting.com
Printed in the USA
LVOW12s2142111214

418448LV00001B/4/P